Scholastic Children's Books
An imprint of Scholastic Ltd
Euston House, 24 Eversholt Street, London, NW1 1DB, UK
Registered office: Westfield Road, Southam, Warwickshire, CV47 0RA
SCHOLASTIC and associated logos are trademarks and/or
registered trademarks of Scholastic Inc.

The Big, Bad Battle of the Bionic Booger Boy Part 2:
The Revenge of the Ridiculous Robo-Boogers
Dedication: For Aidan and Audrey Hamlin

First published in the US by Scholastic Inc, 2003
Copyright © Dav Pilkey, 2003

The Preposterous Plight of the Purple Potty People
Dedication: For Elizabeth "Boom-Boom" Eulberg
Long live the E.E.C.

First published in the US by Scholastic Inc, 2006
Copyright © Dav Pilkey, 2006

The Terrifying Return of Tippy Tinkletrousers
Dedication: For Aaron Mancini

First published in the US by Scholastic Inc, 2012
Copyright © Dav Pilkey, 2012

The right of Dav Pilkey to be identified as the author and illustrator of this work
has been asserted by him.

ISBN 978 1407 19255 0

A CIP catalogue record for this book
is available from the British Library.

Printed by CPI Group (UK) Ltd, Croydon, CR0 4YY
Papers used by Scholastic Children's Books are made
from wood grown in sustainable forests.

1 3 5 7 9 10 8 6 4 2

This is a work of fiction. Names, characters, places, incidents
and dialogues are products of the author's imagination or are used
fictitiously. Any resemblance to actual people, living or dead,
events or locales is entirely coincidental.

www.scholastic.co.uk

CAPTAIN UNDERPANTS AND THE BIG, BAD BATTLE OF THE BIONIC BOOGER BOY PART 2: THE Revenge OF THE RiDICULOUS ROBO·BOOGERS

The Seventh Epic Novel by

DAV PILKEY

SCHOLASTIC

CHAPTERS

Hi everybody, and welcome to the second half of Captain Underpants and the Big, Bad Battle of the Bionic Booger Boy.
This comic book should give you a pretty good update of our story so far. . .

ONE time he alm-ost got killed by a dandyLion.
Help!
So George stole some Super Power Juice from a U.F.O.
and he gave it to him.
Super Power Juice
gLub gLub gLub
and ~~Capta~~ Mr Krupp got Super Powers.
Now he can FLy and StuFF.
Here we go again

Now whenever MR Krupp hears som-body snap there Fingers....
BLah BLah BLah!!!
SNAP
... he TURNS int-o Captain Und-erpants.
Tra-La-Laaa!
And whenever C.U. gets water on his head...
H2O
he turns back into MR Krupp.
BLah BLah Blah!
So Remember!!! Don't snap your Fingers around Mr Krupp!
BUT...
Thats onLy The First Part of our Story......
READ ON!

But he Sneezed at the Last second.
A-A-CHOO!
And he axidentelly got combined with a RoBot--- And his Boogers!
ZAP!
He Became the Bionic Booger Boy.
Im a DumB Nerd!
UH OH
Then one time he coght a cold.
A-CHOO
Then he got mad and Terned into a monster.

Now Melvin and mr KRUPP were safe.
But somthing was wrong with Them.
Im a DUMB Nerd
BLAH BLAH BLAH!
Then The Boogers came to Life and smashed the combine-o-thingy...
CRASH!
... And the chase was on!!!
THE END... OF PART 1

CHAPTER 1
GEORGE AND HAROLD

This is George Beard and Harold Hutchins.
George is the kid on the left with the tie
and the flat-top. Harold is the one on the
right with the T-shirt and the bad haircut.
Remember that now.

This is Mr Krupp, Melvin Sneedly and Sulu the Bionic Hamster. Mr Krupp is the one on the left with the underwear and the bald head. Melvin is the one on the right with the bow tie and the glasses. And Sulu the Bionic Hamster is the hamstery-looking one in the middle with the laser eyeballs,

the Macro-Hydraulic Jump-A-Tronic legs, the Super-Somgobulating mini-Automo-Arms, the virtually indestructible Flexo-Growmonic endoskeleton, and the Twin Turbo-3000 SP5 Kung-Fu Titanium/Lithium Alloy Processor. Remember that now, too.

And these are the Ridiculous Robo-Boogers. Three of the vilest, most disgusting and most terrifying creatures ever to drip across the face of the Earth. Even their *names* were horrible, monstrous monikers, the sound of which would drive madness into the hearts of the bravest of heroes.

If you dare to know their nightmarishly deplorable names, I will tell you. But don't blame me if you have to sleep with a night-light on for the rest of your life.

Their names were (from left to right) Carl, Trixie and Frankenbooger.

See? I told you they were scary names!

Carl, Trixie and Frankenbooger each bellowed out terrifying, ear-piercing screams of unstoppable fury as they chased our heroes down the city streets. Finally, the Robo-Boogers cornered everyone in a dead-end alley. The three phlegmish fiends oozed closer and closer, until at last they leaped towards their prey.

The situation had become so frightening that George, Harold, Melvin and Mr Krupp closed their eyes tightly and waited for the terrifying sounds of their own inevitable demise.

GLoBBle! GLoBBle! GLoBBle!

But instead of hearing inevitable-demisey-type sounds, our heroes heard something quite diferent. You see, at the very last second, Sulu the Bionic Hamster stretched open his Flexo-Growmonic jaw and shoved the three boogery behemoths into his mouth.

Sulu's bionic cheeks swelled to capacity as he raised his furry head towards the sky.

Then, with the force of a lunar shuttle lift-off, Sulu shot the three slimy villains into space.

SPIT-TOOIE! SPIT-TOOIE! SPIT-TOOIE!

The three Ridiculous Robo-Boogers sailed through the sky like cannonballs. In no time at all, they left Earth's atmosphere and began sailing towards Uranus. The terrifying battle was over.

"Wow, that was a really quick story," said Harold. "This is going to be our shortest adventure ever!"

"Ain't *that* the truth!" said George.

CHAPTER 2
IT AIN'T

Unfortunately for George and Harold, their adventure had only just begun. As everyone walked back to school, a confusing argument got underway.

"I want my hamster back," said Mr Krupp.

"*Your* hamster?" said George. "First of all, he's *OUR* hamster now. And second of all, he never belonged to you. He belonged to Melvin."

"I don't care WHO he belongs to," Melvin interrupted. "Hamsters aren't allowed in school . . . especially not in MY SCHOOL! I'm giving all three of you bubs a detention for bringing that furry beast into your classroom!"

"You can't give us a detention," said Harold. "You're just a kid like us!"

Suddenly, Mr and Mrs Sneedly came
running towards them.

"Melvin, you're all right!" cried Mrs
Sneedly.

"We're so happy you're safe, son!" cried
Mr Sneedly.

"Mummy! Poppa!" cried Mr Krupp. He
dashed over to Melvin's parents with open
arms. The sight of a bald, grown man in his
underwear running towards them made Mrs
Sneedly scream in horror.

"Hey, what's the big idea?" yelled
Mr Sneedly.

"It's me, Poppa," cried Mr Krupp. "Don't
you recognize your own son?"

"Get away from us, you – you – you
WEIRDO!" Mrs Sneedly yelled as she hit
Mr Krupp with her handbag.

Melvin ignored the commotion as he
walked past them all and went into
the school.

Melvin stormed upstairs and headed for the school office. Everyone except Miss Anthrope had already gone home for the day, and she was getting ready to leave, too.

"Just where do you think you're going, woman?!!?" shouted Melvin.

Miss Anthrope turned and stared in shock at the fourth grader standing behind her.

"What did you JUST *SAY*?!!?" she cried
in a voice that was rapidly becoming a
scream. "Who – WHO DO YOU THINK
YOU ARE?!!?"

"I'm the guy who's gonna fire you if
you don't get me my coffee . . . *NOW*!"
yelled Melvin.

Normally, school secretaries don't have the authority to hang a child from a coat hook by his underwear, but today had been a particularly stressful day for Miss Anthrope. She had been covered in snot, carried through town by a rampaging robotic monster and (worst of all) forced to chaperone an elementary school field trip. Now it was payback time.

CHAPTER 3

MR MELVIN AND KRUPPY THE KID

Miss Anthrope collected her things and left for home, grumbling under her breath as she passed George and Harold in the hallway. The two boys could hear Melvin's angry shouts coming from down the hall, so they went to the office to investigate.

While they were getting Melvin off the hook, Mr Krupp ran into the office, sweaty and out of breath.

"You guys have gotta help me," he cried. "My mum and dad are trying to kill me! Has the world gone MAD?"

"Relax, Einstein," said George calmly, "and put on some clothes!" George and Harold had already figured out what was going on, so they tried to explain the situation to Melvin and Mr Krupp.

"You see," said Harold, "after you guys got morphed together by the Combine-O-Tron 2000, we switched the batteries around and separated you. But for some strange reason, it switched your *brains* around. Now Mr Krupp's brain is inside Melvin's body, and Melvin's brain is inside Mr Krupp's body."

"That's a buncha BUNK!" yelled Melvin.

"Take a look and see for yourselves," said George. He pulled a full-length mirror in front of Mr Krupp and Melvin. They looked at themselves in astonishment.

"I'm – I'm a kid again," said the guy who looked like Melvin but had Mr Krupp's brain.

"And I'm old and fat and bald and ugly," cried the guy who looked like Mr Krupp but had Melvin's brain. "And I have bad breath and creepy nose hairs and—"

"HEY!" yelled the guy who looked like Melvin but had Mr Krupp's brain.

At this point, you might be saying to yourself, "Dang, this book is getting confusing!" Now don't worry, this'll all get cleared up by the end of chapter 17. But for now, let's rename the two characters who have the right brains in the wrong bodies, shall we? Let's call the guy who looks like Mr. Krupp (but has Melvin Sneedly's brain) "Mr Melvin". And we'll call the kid who looks like Melvin Sneedly (but has Mr Krupp's brain) "Kruppy the Kid".

Please refer to the handy X-ray chart below in case you get mixed-up:

CHAPTER 4
THINGS GET WORSE

Kruppy the Kid climbed up into his chair and demanded to know what was going to be done about this mix-up.

"I could solve this problem right away if I still had my Combine-O-Tron 2000," said Mr Melvin sheepishly, "but it got smashed in the last book."

"Well start building a new one, bub!" shouted Kruppy the Kid.

"OK," whined Mr Melvin, "but it'll take about six months."

"SIX MONTHS?!!?" screamed Kruppy the Kid. "I can't go around looking like a kid for six months! I've got a school to run, buster!"

"Sorry," Mr Melvin whimpered, "but building a cellular combiner is extremely difficult. It takes time. It's not easy like building a robot, or a time machine, or a Photo-Atomic Trans-Somgobulating Yectofantriplutoniczanziptomiser."

"Hey, wait a second," said George. "Did you just say that building a time machine was *easy*?"

"Yeah," said Mr Melvin. "It just takes a day or two. Why?"

"Well, why don't you just build a time machine?" asked George. "Then you can go back in time to before the Combine-O-Tron 2000 got smashed, grab it, and bring it back to the present time."

Mr Melvin thought for a moment, and then his eyes lit up. "I've got it!" he said, snapping his fingers. "I'll build a time machine, then go back in time to before the Combine-O-Tron 2000 got smashed, grab it, and bring it back to the – hey, what the heck is *HE* doing?!!?"

Everyone turned and looked at Kruppy the Kid, who had just stripped down to his underwear and was now tying a red curtain around his neck.

"OH, NO!" screamed George. "GET SOME WATER!!! GET SOME WATER!!!"

Harold ran out to the drinking fountain,
but he was too late. Kruppy the Kid shouted
a triumphant "Tra-La-Laaaaa!", then turned
and flew out the window.

CHAPTER 5
THINGS GET WORSER

"Did – did you guys just see that?" cried Mr Melvin. "I just – I mean, Kruppy the Kid just flew out the window! He FLEW!"

"Yeah, we know," said George with a sigh.

"That's – that's *amazing*!" cried Mr Melvin. "He must think he's Captain Underpants or something. Or . . . or could it be? Could our principal really BE Captain Underpants?"

"Well, *duh*!" said Harold.

"But Mr Krupp doesn't look anything
like Captain Underpants," said Mr Melvin
frantically. "Captain Underpants is bald! And
Mr Krupp usually has hair. Hey! I know!
Maybe Mr Krupp wears a toupee?"

"I thought you were supposed to be in the
'gifted' stream," said George.

"But – but how can he fly? Where did he
get his super powers?" asked Mr Melvin.

"It's a long story," said Harold.

Mr Melvin calmed down a bit, walked
confidently across the room, and sat in the
principal's chair. He leaned back and smiled a
devilish grin. "Well, why don't you go ahead
and tell me all about it?" said Mr Melvin.
"I've got all the time in the world!"

CHAPTER 6

THINGS GET WORSEREST

George and Harold had no choice but to come clean. They told Mr Melvin the whole story of Captain Underpants: how they had hypnotized Mr Krupp, how he drank the alien Super Power Juice, and how his super powers must have somehow got transferred into Melvin's body along with Mr Krupp's brain.

While George and Harold were talking, the smile on Mr Melvin's face grew wider and wider, and eviler and eviler.

"What're you smiling about?" said George. "This is SERIOUS!"

"Yeah," said Harold. "We're all in big trouble if we don't switch things back to normal!"

"Correction," said Mr Melvin. "*YOU* guys are in big trouble. All my troubles are OVER. I, Melvin Sneedly, am gonna get back into my old body, but KEEP those super powers for myself. I'm gonna become the world's first super-powered kid!"

"Hey, you can't do that," said Harold.

"*I can do whatever I want,*" snapped Mr Melvin. "I'm in charge now. I look just like the principal, so I'm gonna make the rules, and you guys are gonna follow them – or else!"

"Or else what?" George demanded.

"Or *else*," snarled Mr Melvin, "I'll order your teachers to give you guys twelve hours of homework every night for the next eight years!"

That shut George and Harold up.

Mr Melvin's first order of the day was for George and Harold to make a new comic book about the world's first super-powered kid, Melvin Sneedly.

"Give me a really cool name," said Mr Melvin, "like *Big Melvin* or *Mystery Melvin*. . ."

"MYSTERY MELVIN???" said George and Harold in disbelief.

". . .and make up a story where I defeat Captain Underpants and become the world's greatest superhero. And you better not make me look stupid, either!" Mr Melvin shouted.

"But we can't make a comic book
right now," cried Harold. "We've gotta
chase after Captain Kruppy the . . . uh
. . . Underpants Kid."

"You can chase after him all you want,"
said Mr Melvin, "*AFTER* you make that
comic book. Now get going! I've got a time
machine to build."

CHAPTER 7

THE PURPLE POTTY

Mr Melvin went out and bought all the things he needed to build his time machine. Now he just needed a *place* to build it. He wanted someplace quiet and private. Someplace empty and secluded. A room that nobody ever, EVER used.

"I've got it!" he cried. "Our school library!"

The library at Jerome Horwitz Elementary School had once been a wonderful place of knowledge and learning. But a few years back, the librarian, Miss Singerbrains, had begun banning most of the books. Now the library was filled only with rows of empty bookshelves and posters that warned of the potential subversive dangers of reading. It was the perfect place to hatch an evil plan.

Mr Melvin pushed his cart into the dusty, cobwebby room and flicked on the lights.

"Welcome, sir," said Miss Singerbrains. "Have you come to check out the book?"

"Uh, nooo," said Mr Melvin. "I need to find a large box, like a phone booth or something."

"There's a purple portable potty down in the basement," said Miss Singerbrains.

"That'll do," Mr Melvin said. "Go get it for me."

"I can't carry that thing up three flights of stairs all by myself," cried Miss Singerbrains.

"All right, all right," said Mr Melvin. "I'll help you."

Mr Melvin supervised while Miss Singerbrains carried the heavy potty to the top of the treacherous steps.

"Good job," said Mr Melvin. "Now go clean out your desk. You're fired."

"FIRED?!!?" cried Miss Singerbrains. "What for?"

"Uh . . . for the rest of your life," said Mr Melvin.

CHAPTER 8

MEANWHILE, BACK IN OUTER SPACE. . .

A team of scientists working at the Piqua Order of Professional Space and Interplanetary Explorers (POOPSIE) were on their way to investigate the planet Uranus, when they came across something that was very strange.

Major "Buzz" Tomski and his crew had just discovered a bizarre cluster of what appeared to be robots and toilets resting on the planet's surface.

The astronauts were so busy looking at their monitor that they didn't notice the three slimy, squishy, boogery thingies speeding towards their spaceship.

CHAPTER 9

GROUND CONTROL TO MAJOR TOMSKI

Suddenly, a very concerned voice came across the POOPSIE space phone. "What's going on up there, bub?" asked Ground Control.

"W-we're OK," said Major Tomski as he unzipped the cockpit's window screen for a better look. "But it appears our ship has just been splattered by three unidentified squishy objects!"

"That does it!" said Ground Control. "This mission is just getting too strange. I want you guys to turn that ship around and come on back home."

"Will do," said Major Tomski. He pushed in the clutch, shifted the ship into reverse, and in no time at all, the POOPSIE shuttle was headed back to Earth . . .

. . . with three giggling stowaways hanging on for the long ride home.

CHAPTER 10
MEAN MR MELVIN

The next day, Mr Melvin was putting the finishing touches on his time machine when he heard cries of laughter out in the hallway.

He opened the library door and saw a
group of third graders happily reading
George and Harold's newest comic book.
Mr Melvin stomped down the hall, grabbed
the comic out of their hands, and gasped
in horror.

"WHAT THE —?!!?" he screamed as he
glared at the comic book's cover.

A-Ha! I gots you!
O.K. Do watever you want But Please Dont Dunk me in the Lake
HUH?
You can KiLL me But Please Dont Dunk me in The Lake I Prey it!
OH yeah? WeLL may-Be I WiLL Dunk you in The Lake.
OH Hevens No!
ILL SHow You!!!
No way!
The Lake
Ha Ha Ha! Get Ready
AW maan!
Hey! What the???

CHAPTER 12
MAD MR MELVIN

Mr Melvin was furious. He marched into the office and turned on the school intercom.

"George Beard and Harold Hutchins," he shouted over the loudspeakers, "meet Mr Melv – er, I mean, Mr *Krupp* in the school library RIGHT NOW!"

"We have a library?" said George.

After about twenty minutes of searching, George and Harold finally came across a room they had never seen before. They entered cautiously, stepping quietly past rows and rows of empty bookshelves until they met up with Mr Melvin.

"I told you guys to give me a cool name and not to make me look stupid!" Mr Melvin screamed, clutching their comic book in his sweaty hand.

"Oops," said George. "I thought you said to give you a stupid name and NOT to make you look cool."

"Yeah," said Harold. "It was an honest misunderstanding."

Mr Melvin threw the comic book to the ground, then led George and Harold over to the Purple Potty.

"Remember when I had that great idea to build a time machine?" asked Mr Melvin.

"Actually," said George, "that was *my*—"

"Well, here it is," Mr Melvin interrupted triumphantly. "And you two smarty-pantses are going to test it out for me!"

"Huh?" said Harold.

"I'm sending you kids back in time to the day before yesterday," Mr Melvin said. "And you better not return until you've got my Combine-O-Tron 2000."

"Cool," said George. "I've always wanted to travel through time."

Mr Melvin had a great deal of instructions for George and Harold before they left on their journey. And though the instructions were quite boring, it would have benefited the boys if they had paid attention instead of switching the letters around on a nearby bulletin board.

Mr Melvin spoke at length about the workings of the time machine and the proper etiquette of time travel.

"You must be very careful that nobody sees you on your journey," Mr Melvin said. "If they do, just zap them with my new invention, the Forgetchamacallit 2000."

CHECK OUT OUR SCHOOL'S BIG INTERNET WEBSITE AT WWW.JHES.COM!

FAKE COMBINE-O-TRON 2000

"This will erase everything in their short-term memory, and they won't remember ever seeing you." Mr Melvin had also built a fake Combine-O-Tron 2000 to switch with the real one.

Finally, Mr Melvin gave George and Harold a very important warning: "Whatever you do, it is very important that you don't use this time machine two days in a row. It needs to cool off *every other day*, or else it might open up an oppozo-dimensional reality rift that could destroy the entire planet."

PURPLE POTTY CO.

FORGETCHA-MACALLIT 2000

George and Harold started laughing at their new message on the bulletin board.

"HEY!" Mr Melvin shouted. "Have you kids even heard *one* word I've said?"

"Yeah, yeah, yeah," said George. "We gotta switch the thing with the thingy!"

"And if somebody sees us," said Harold, "we'll zap 'em with the whichamajiggy."

"Don't worry, we *got* it!" said George.

George and Harold stepped into the
Purple Potty as Mr Melvin closed the door
behind them. Harold set the controller for
the day before yesterday. Then George
pulled the chain. Suddenly, there was a
brilliant flash of green light, and the Purple
Potty disappeared.

CHAPTER 13

THE DAY BEFORE YESTERDAY

After a few moments of flashing lights, everything became quiet. Harold opened the potty door and peeked out into the darkened library. Cautiously the two time travellers stepped to the library window and looked out. There they saw Melvin's father, Mr Sneedly, zapping the Bionic Booger Boy with a blast from the Combine-O-Tron 2000.

"Been there," said George.

"Done that," said Harold.

In the corner, George and Harold found
a coat and hat, which belonged to Miss
Singerbrains. Immediately, they thought
of a plan. Harold put on the coat and hat,
and climbed on to George's shoulders.

"I sure hope this disguise works," said
Harold.

"It better," said George. "We can't risk
letting them recognize us."

Soon George and Harold were at the scene of the action. Mr Sneedly had just fired the Combine-O-Tron 2000 a second time, and now the boys were ready to make their move.

"Um, excuse me, Mr Sneedly," said Harold, trying very hard to sound like a grown-up. "I'd like to present unto you *The Most Brilliantest Science Guy of the Whole Wide World Award*."

"Really?" cried Mr Sneedly. "It's always been my dream to win that award!"

"But first," said Harold, "I'd like to have a look at that Combine-O-Thingy."

"OK," said Mr. Sneedly. He handed Harold the Combine-O-Tron 2000 and smiled proudly.

"Um . . ." said Harold. "I need to look at it behind those bushes over there."

Harold and George wobbled over to the bushes, unbuttoned their coat and switched the two Combine-O-Trons. Then they wobbled back and handed the fake Combine-O-Tron 2000 to Mr Sneedly.

"Um . . . everything seems to be in order," said Harold. "But before we present the award, we'd like to get a photo of you."

"Who's *we*?" asked Mr Sneedly.

"Uh . . . I mean *I'd* like to get a photo of you," said Harold nervously.

George stuck his hand out of the coat and held up the Forgetchamacallit 2000.

"Say cheese," said Harold.

Mr Sneedly looked down in shock at George's hand. Then George pressed the button.

FLASH!

Suddenly, Mr Sneedly forgot everything
that had just happened. Dazed and confused,
he stumbled back and rejoined his wife just
in time for the Robo-Boogers to come to life
and smash the fake Combine-O-Tron 2000.

Meanwhile, George and Harold were running with all their might back to the library, carrying the *real* Combine-O-Tron 2000.

"That was SO easy!" laughed George.

"Yeah!" said Harold. "We sure got lucky this time!"

But when they reached the library door, George and Harold discovered that they hadn't been quite so lucky after all.

CHAPTER 14
MISS SINGERBRAINS

"What the heck is going on here?" shouted Miss Singerbrains. "I just got back from the restroom and found a *portable potty* in my library!"

"Harold!" said George. "Zap her with the Forgetcha-thingy – quick!"

"Nobody's zapping anybody with anything!" shouted Miss Singerbrains. She grabbed the Forgetchamacallit 2000 out of Harold's hands and yanked the Combine-O-Tron 2000 out of George's hands.

"I'm taking these things to the police right now!" she said. "Maybe they can sort this mess out!"

Miss Singerbrains marched downstairs
to the parking lot, got in her car, and began
driving to the police station.

"Well," said Harold, "we'll never catch up
with her now!"

"Sure we will!" said George. "All we need
are some *wings*!"

CHAPTER 15

65 MILLION YEARS BEFORE THE DAY BEFORE YESTERDAY

George and Harold grabbed a box of crackers off Miss Singerbrains's desk. Then the two friends stepped inside the Purple Potty and closed the door. Quickly, George reset the controls and pulled down on the chain.

A flash of green light lit up the room, and the Purple Potty vanished.

Suddenly, George and Harold were transported back in time to the late Cretaceous period of the Mesozoic era, a time when dinosaurs ruled the Earth.

Cautiously, George and Harold peeked out of the Purple Potty, which was now nestled precariously in the branches of a tall tree.

"Here chickie, chickie, chickie!" called George.

"Polly want a cracker?" called Harold as he tossed a handful of crackers into the air.

Suddenly, the two boys were swarmed by hungry pterodactyls.

Before long, a friendly-looking pterodactyl (a Quetzalcoatlus to be exact) swooped down and grabbed some crackers from Harold's hand.

"Aww, look," said Harold. "He likes me!"

"Great," said George. "Let's get him into the time machine and get out of here!"

Carefully, Harold took the pterodactyl in his arms and carried him into the Purple Potty. Then, the boys closed the door behind them, reset the controls, and pulled down on the chain.

Suddenly, George and Harold (and their new reptilian pal) were transported forward in time to the day before yesterday.

The door of the time machine swung open, and the three friends sailed out of the Purple Potty, through the library window, and up over the town.

George looked down on the city streets until finally he located Miss Singerbrains's car. "There she is!" George cried.

"I sure love our new pterodactyl," said Harold. "I'm gonna name him Crackers."

"Don't give him a name," said George. "We're not keeping him. We're just borrowing him!"

George, Harold and Crackers swooped down and landed on Miss Singerbrains's car, which was parked at a traffic light.

Miss Singerbrains screamed in horror.

"Wait!" cried George. "There's no reason to be afraid. You're just *dreaming*!"

"I'm dreaming?" asked Miss Singerbrains.

"Sure. Think about it," said Harold. "Purple Potties appearing out of nowhere . . . kids running around with laser zappers . . . pterosaurs landing on your car . . . this stuff only happens in dreams."

"Gosh, you're right," said Miss Singerbrains. "But it all seems so real."

"Well, trust us," said George. "In a few minutes you won't remember any of it."

Before long, George, Harold and Miss Singerbrains were all gliding back to school with their good pal Crackers. The Combine-O-Tron 2000 and the Forgetchamacallit 2000 were safe once again.

Soon, they arrived back at the library.

"I'll keep an eye on Miss Singerbrains," said George. "You take that pterodactyl back where we found him."

"Aww, can't we keep him?" asked Harold.

"No," said George sternly. "He belongs in his own time. Now take him back!"

"Aww, *maaaan*," said Harold.

Sadly, Harold carried Crackers into the
Purple Potty and closed the door. After a few
seconds, the time machine disappeared in
a flash of green light.

A half hour later, another flash of green light filled the room, and the Purple Potty was back.

"What took you so long?" asked George.

"Ummm . . . nothing," said Harold.

"Did you have any trouble taking Crackers back to his home?" asked George.

"Ummmm . . . not really," said Harold.

"You *DID* take him back to his home, didn't you?" asked George.

"Ummmmm . . . sure," said Harold, though he didn't *sound* very sure.

Quickly, George zapped Miss Singerbrains with the Forgetchamacallit 2000 and jumped into the Purple Potty. Then, with a quick flash of green light, they were gone.

CHAPTER 16

BACK TO THE PRESENT

Mr Melvin was very happy to see his Purple Potty return to him . . . and even happier to see his beloved Combine-O-Tron 2000.

"Now all I need," he said with a sneer, "is to find Captain Underpants."

Fortunately, Captain Underpants (who you'll probably remember looked just like Melvin Sneedly) wasn't too far away. *Unfortunately*, he had spent the last two days getting himself into trouble.

First, he started off by annoying some old ladies. Captain Underpants had been helping them cross the street when he heard a little girl crying for her kitten, which was stuck in a tree.

Captain Underpants rescued the kitty but forgot about the old ladies.

"Hey!" shouted one of the old ladies. "That flying kid just left us up here in this tree!"

"I'm gonna get that kid if it's the last thing I do!" said the other old lady.

Next, Captain Underpants was soaring
above the football field when he encountered
an unidentified flying object. It was made
of brown leather and had white stitching on
the side.

"Hmmm," said Captain Underpants. "This
could be a dangerous UFO!" He grabbed it
and flew down to the football field, where,
oddly, the school's football team was having
a big game.

"I don't want anybody to panic!" Captain Underpants shouted. "But I just captured this UFO. I'm going to take it to the moon, where it can be safely destroyed."

Suddenly, the players from the visiting team tackled Captain Underpants, which cost the home team fifty metres . . . and the game.

"That kid just made us lose our biggest game of the year!" shouted Mr Meaner.

"I'm gonna get that kid if it's the last thing I do," snarled the quarterback.

Finally, Captain Underpants got on the bad side of some skateboarders in the park. He had politely pointed out the *No Skateboarding* signs, but the skateboarders refused to go away. So Captain Underpants had no choice but to snap their skateboards in half with his kung-fu kicking action.

Then it was spankings for everyone!

"Dude!" cried one of the skateboarders. "That little dude just, like, duded our dudeboards."

"Dude," said another skateboarder. "I'm gonna dude that dude if it's the last dude I dude!"

CHAPTER 17

THE BIG SWITCHEROONIE

Mr Melvin ordered George and Harold to stick their heads out the window and call for Captain Underpants. Soon, the Waistband Warrior appeared.

Mr Melvin welcomed the caped hero inside and asked him to pose for a photo.

"Why, I'd be delighted," said Captain Underpants.

"Great," said Mr Melvin. "Put these clothes on and stand over there!"

At first, Captain Underpants was reluctant to put on clothes, but he finally agreed.

Mr Melvin, who had worked all afternoon reconfiguring the Combine-O-Tron 2000, pressed the start button, then ran and stood beside Captain Underpants. Suddenly, two glowing lasers began encoding the DNA of the two subjects it was about to combine.

Then, a burst of brilliant grey light shot out of the Combine-O-Tron 2000 and formed a ball of energy between Captain Underpants and Mr Melvin. They both slid together into the grey light and formed a giant glob of fleshy goo.

The newly reconfigured Combine-O-Tron 2000 then switched polarities and began the process of separating the two human elements. The grey ball of light slowly changed to a lovely shade of pink.

Suddenly, there was a blinding flash of light, a quick puff of smoke, and it was all over. Everybody's brains were back where they belonged.

"Wow, that sure is a weird camera," said Captain Underpants (who now looked exactly like Captain Underpants). "Can I take these clothes off now? They're bad for my image."

"Go right ahead," said Melvin Sneedly (who now looked exactly like Melvin Sneedly).

Finally, it looked as if everything was back to normal. But as we all know, looks can be deceiving.

CHAPTER 18

THE RETURN OF THE RIDICULOUS ROBO-BOOGERS

Just then, the POOPSIE space shuttle landed at Piqua International Airport. It wasn't the smoothest of landings, due to the fact that three robotic boogers had just eaten most of the shuttle's tailfin and nearly all of its rocket thrusters.

Major Tomski and his crew had barely escaped with their lives.

Inside the school library, Captain
Underpants heard the astronauts' panicked
cries coming from the airport.

"This looks like a job for me!" he shouted.
And with a mighty "Tra-La-Laaaaa!", he
leaped out the window . . .

. . . and fell three storeys to the ground.

George and Harold screamed and ran downstairs.

"Captain Underpants!" cried George. "Are you OK?"

"Speak to us!" cried Harold.

Captain Underpants slowly lifted his head in confusion.

"Mummy . . ." he said weakly, ". . . my train went swimming in the piano."

Meanwhile, over at Piqua International Airport, Carl, Trixie and Frankenbooger had just finished eating the space shuttle and were now starting to munch on the control tower. The three globby gluttons grew bigger and bigger with every enormous bite.

"C'mon, Captain Underpants," cried George. "You've gotta save those people!"

"But I forgot how to fly," Captain Underpants said sheepishly.

"You didn't forget," laughed Melvin Sneedly, who was now floating above their heads. "You've just LOST your super powers. But don't worry, they've been safely transferred into *MY* body. Now *I'm* the world's greatest superhero!"

"Melvin," cried George, "those Robo-Boogers came back to Earth! They're attacking people at the airport! You've gotta help those people!"

"I'm not doing a thing until you guys change that comic book!" Melvin said. "And you better make me look cool this time!"

"But there's no time," cried Harold. "Those people need your help NOW!"

"Well, you better start drawing then, art boy!" said Melvin.

CHAPTER 19

NEVER UNDERESTIMATE THE POWER OF UNDERWEAR

George and Harold begged Melvin to use his super powers to save the day, but Melvin continued to refuse. Finally, Captain Underpants stepped in.

"You may have taken away my super powers," the Waistband Warrior said, "but I still have the power of underwear on my side. And nobody can take that away from me!"

Captain Underpants turned and ran towards the airport.

"Melvin," cried George frantically, "if you don't do something, those boogers are gonna *kill* Mr Krupp!"

"That's not *my* fault," said Melvin. "You're the ones who wrote that stupid comic book about me. Now change it, or ELSE!"

George and Harold looked at each other. Their choice was simple: either fight with Captain Underpants (and probably die), or give in to the dark side and live.

The two boys turned and ran to the airport.

CHAPTER 20
BOOGER BRUNCH

George and Harold quickly caught up with Captain Underpants. Soon, they were all at the airport witnessing the carnage of the Ridiculous Robo-Boogers.

Captain Underpants shouted out
a triumphant "Tra-La-Laaaaa!" from below.
Suddenly, the three Robo-Boogers turned
towards the familiar-sounding voice. Quickly,
their laser-guided eyeballs zoomed in on
three of the heroes who had made their lives
so miserable back in chapter 1. Immediately,
the Robo-Boogers leaped at George, Harold
and Captain Underpants . . . and the chase
was on . . . again!

CHAPTER 21
CORNERED

The Robo-Boogers continued chasing
George, Harold and Captain Underpants,
until at last the three frightened friends
were cornered at a local shopping centre.

In a desperate attempt to save themselves, the three brave heroes began taking items from the outside sales bins and throwing them at the snarling beasts.

George grabbed a pair of low-fat tennis shoes and tossed them at Trixie. Trixie gobbled them up.

Harold found a delicious tube of wild-cherry-flavored haemorrhoid ointment and flung it at Frankenbooger.

Frankenbooger swallowed it whole.

YTHING
XCEPT
SOFTENER
R NON-FABRIC SOFTENING NEEDS

SALE

Captain Underpants picked up a
genetically-modified, organic-orange-
flavoured orange and chucked it at Carl.
Carl chewed it up with a smug grin.

Suddenly, Carl's laser eyes grew incredibly large. The haughty smile on his face turned into a panicked gasp as the wet, gooshy snot that covered his body began to dry up and crumble. Huge, crispy booglets shot off his smouldering robotic endoskeleton like green popcorn.

"What's going on?" cried Harold.

"It's the *oranges*!" cried George. "It's gotta be the vitamin C in these oranges. It's combatting the cold and flu that caused those boogers to turn evil!"

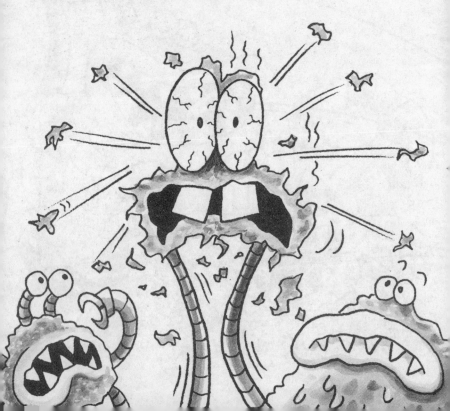

Carl thrashed around brutally as more and more of his disintegrating body cracked off and fell to the ground. Finally, the lights in his panic-stricken laser eyes slowly went out. He stumbled over and crashed horribly into the parking lot. Carl – was dead.

CHAPTER 22
VITAMIN C YOU LATER

George, Harold and Captain Underpants
quickly began chucking oranges at Trixie
and Frankenbooger. But the two remaining
Robo-Boogers had got wise to the power of
vitamin C. They ducked, jumped, dodged
and darted, doing whatever they could to
avoid being hit by the deadly oranges.

"Hey! I've got an idea," said Captain
Underpants. He grabbed two crates of
oranges and ran off, while George and Harold
continued flinging fruit ferociously.

"Where does he think *he's* going?" said
George.

"I don't know," said Harold, "but his idea
better work. We're running out of oranges!"

Soon, George and Harold were down to their last two oranges. They threw them as hard as they could, but alas, the potent projectiles missed their terrifying targets.

Trixie and Frankenbooger grabbed George and Harold and dangled them above their gigantic mouths.

"Well," said George, "it looks like this is the end."

"Yep," said Harold. "It was nice knowing you, pal."

Suddenly, the Robo-Boogers heard a familiar "Tra-La-Laaaaa!" coming from somewhere over on the next page.

The repulsive Robo-Boogers dropped George and Harold, and stomped over to page 130. There they found Captain Underpants standing at the top of a large novelty toilet on the roof of John's House of Toilets. He was shouting, "Tra-La-Laaaaa!" and doing a very annoying dance, which made the Robo-Boogers very, very angry.

JOHN'S HOUSE OF TOILETS

We'll BOWL you OVER!

CHAPTER 23

THE UNDERPANTS DANCE (IN FLIP-O-RAMA™)

You've tried the Twist,
mastered the Macarena,
and figured out
the Funky Chicken. . .

Now it's time to learn the most
annoying dance ever:
the Underpants Dance.

It's sure to irritate parents,
teachers, evil villains
and kids of all ages!

Just follow the easy steps
in this chapter, and learn
the Underpants Dance today!!!

PILKEY® BRAND
D·RAMA

HERE'S HOW IT WORKS!

STEP 1
First, place your *left* hand inside the dotted lines marked "LEFT HAND HERE". Hold the book open *flat*.

STEP 2
Grasp the *right-hand* page with your right thumb and index finger (inside the dotted lines marked "RIGHT THUMB HERE").

STEP 3
Now *quickly* flip the right-hand page back and forth until the picture appears to be *animated*.

FLIP-O-RAMA 1

(pages 135 and 137)

Remember, flip *only* page 135.
While you are flipping, be sure you
can see the picture on page 135
and the one on page 137.
If you flip quickly, the two
pictures will start to look like
<u>one</u> *animated* picture.

For extra fun, try humming
a stupid song and flipping to the beat!

LEFT HAND HERE

STEP 1:
THE WEDGIE
WIGGLE

RIGHT
THUMB
HERE

STEP 1:
THE WEDGIE
WIGGLE

FLIP-O-RAMA 2

(pages 139 and 141)

Remember, flip *only* page 139.
While you are flipping, be sure you
can see the picture on page 139
and the one on page 141.
If you flip quickly, the two
pictures will start to look like
<u>one</u> *animated* picture.

For extra fun, try humming
a stupid song and flipping to the beat!

LEFT HAND HERE

STEP 2:
THE TOILET-TOP
TANGO

RIGHT
THUMB
HERE

STEP 2:
THE TOILET-TOP TANGO

FLIP-O-RAMA 3

(pages 143 and 145)

Remember, flip *only* page 143.
While you are flipping, be sure you
can see the picture on page 143
and the one on page 145.
If you flip quickly, the two
pictures will start to look like
<u>one</u> *animated* picture.

For extra fun, try humming
a stupid song and flipping to the beat!

LEFT HAND HERE

STEP 3:
THE WAISTBAND
WATUSI

RIGHT
THUMB
HERE

STEP 3:
THE WAISTBAND
WATUSI

FLIP-O-RAMA 4

(pages 147 and 149)

Remember, flip *only* page 147.
While you are flipping, be sure you
can see the picture on page 147
and the one on page 149.
If you flip quickly, the two
pictures will start to look like
<u>one</u> *animated* picture.

For extra fun, try humming
a stupid song and flipping to the beat!

LEFT HAND HERE

STEP 4:
THE BIG BUTT
BOOGIE

RIGHT
THUMB
HERE

STEP 4:
THE BIG BUTT
BOOGIE

CHAPTER 24
SQUISHIES, PART 2

Trixie and Frankenbooger had seen enough. They couldn't stand to watch Captain Underpants doing that stupid dance one second longer. So they pushed down on the seat of the large novelty toilet to hoist themselves up on the roof.

Unfortunately for Trixie and Franken-booger, they had been so irritated by the Underpants Dance that they hadn't noticed the two crates of oranges placed carefully under the gigantic toilet seat. When they pressed down, the pressure of the toilet seat crushed the orange crates, spraying delicious, vitaminey orange juice all over their big, bad, boogery bodies.

George, Harold, and Captain Underpants watched as their monstrous archenemies began decomposing before their very eyes.

"What happened to them?" asked Harold.

"I gave them a *Squishy*," said Captain Underpants. "It's the latest fad."

The Robo-Boogers jerked around wildly as the quickly drying snot crumbled off of their smoking robotic endoskeletons. Then, after a few minutes of spinning and screaming, they slowly tumbled to the ground in two metallic heaps.

Trixie and Frankenbooger — were dead.

CHAPTER 25
"BIG MELVIN"

Soon, Ingrid Ashley from Channel 4
Eyewitness News arrived at the scene.
"How did you manage to destroy the Robo-
Boogers?" she asked.

"I'll answer that," said Melvin Sneedly, as
he swooped in front of the cameras. He was
robed in some old drapes that he had tied
around his neck at the last minute, and he
looked quite silly.

"I, *Big Melvin*, fought those monsters
with my mighty super powers," Melvin fibbed.
"Then I destroyed them with my super-smart
brain!"

"No, you didn't," said Harold.

"You weren't even here!" said George.

"Don't listen to those guys," said Melvin. "I, *Big Melvin*, am the real hero here." Melvin flew above the two defeated Robo-Boogers and used his new laser eye-beams to burn the letters *B* and *M* in front of the dead creatures.

"Just like Zorro," said Big Melvin, "I shall sign my initials on all of my heroic handiwork. From now on, whenever you see a big *BM*, you'll think of me!"

"That's funny," said George. "Big *BM*s have always made me think of you."

Big Melvin flew over to Captain Underpants and grabbed him by the arm.

"Now," said Big Melvin, "the entire world shall bear witness to the humiliating defeat of Captain Underpants!"

Suddenly, George and Harold got an idea. They turned and ran back to the school while Big Melvin continued to threaten Captain Underpants.

"I command you to bow down to me," shouted Big Melvin.

"*Never!*" said Captain Underpants.

"You SHALL bow down to me!" Big Melvin yelled.

"*I SHAN'T!*" cried Captain Underpants.

"Then," said Big Melvin, as he untied the drapes around his neck, "you will feel the power of my wrath!"

CHAPTER 26
THE DRAPES OF WRATH

Big Melvin held his drapes tightly, then smacked Captain Underpants in the tushie with them.

"I command you to deny underwear and accept the power of Big Melvin!" he shouted.

"No *way, Pedro*!" cried Captain Underpants.

Big Melvin smacked Captain Underpants again.

"Bow down to me," he commanded, "and
I shall spare your life!"

"Aww, go jump off a duck!" said Captain
Underpants defiantly.

Suddenly, George and Harold returned to the scene, out of breath, and hiding something behind their backs.

"Hey, Big Melvin!" shouted George, huffing and puffing.

"What?" yelled Big Melvin.

Harold pulled the Combine-O-Tron 2000 out from behind his back and aimed it at Melvin and Captain Underpants.

"You shouldn't leave your toys lyin' around in the library, bub!" he said slyly.

Melvin shrieked in horror as Harold pulled the trigger.

BLAZZZZT!

A blinding flash of grey light shot out of the Combine-O-Tron 2000, surrounding Melvin and Captain Underpants and squishing them together.

George had reset the controller to combine them both, transfer the super powers back to Captain Underpants, then separate them.

"I sure hope this works," said Harold.

"Me, too," said George.

CHAPTER 27

TO MAKE A LONG STORY SHORT

It did.

BONK

CHAPTER 28

WITH BIG UNDERWEAR COMES BIG RESPONSIBILITY

Big Melvin fell to the ground with a thud. Immediately, Captain Underpants began floating in the air.

"Hey!" cried the good Captain. "I've got my super powers back! I knew that underwear would never let me down!"

George turned and zapped the Channel 4 Eyewitness News team with the Forgetchamacallit 2000.

FLASH!

Suddenly, the Channel 4 Eyewitness News team (as well as everyone at home watching the story unfold on Channel 4 Eyewitness News) immediately forgot what had just happened.

The horror was over, everything was back to normal, and everyone was happy.

Well . . . everyone except Big Melvin, that is.

"*Waaaaaah!*" sobbed Melvin. "I want my super powers back!"

"Aww, quit your whining, bub!" said George. "You've been a total jerk for the last two books. You should just be happy that you didn't get your comeuppance!"

CHAPTER 29

COMEUPPANCE SEE ME SOMETIME

Soon, a crowd gathered and began to recognize Melvin.

"Hey!" cried Miss Anthrope. "That's the little squirt who said he was going to *fire* me!"

"There he is!" shouted a couple of very angry old ladies. "That's the little brat who left us up in a tree."

"He made us lose the big game," cried the entire football team simultaneously.

"Dudes," yelled one of the skateboarders, "that's the little dude who duded our dudeboards a few dudes ago!"

"Heh, heh," laughed Melvin nervously. "Maybe I'll just go home now."

"*Get him!*" shouted the old ladies.

"AAAAAH!" screamed Melvin as he ran away, followed closely by a large group of very angry people.

CHAPTER 30
HAROLD'S SURPRISE

As Melvin and his angry mob ran off into the sunset, George and Harold had just one last thing to deal with.

A quick squirt of water to Captain Underpants's face was all it took to bring him back to his Kruppy old self.

"Well, that takes care of that," said George, and the two boys walked back to their tree house.

As George climbed up the ladder to the
tree house, Harold became quite fidgety.

"Ummmmmm . . ." said Harold nervously,
"there's something I should probably tell
you, George."

But when George reached the top of
the ladder and looked inside the tree house,
no explanation was necessary.

"Hey!" said George. "I thought you told me you took Crackers back to his home."

"I did," said Harold. "Back to his *new* home."

"*Harold*," said George sternly, "we can't keep a pet pterodactyl. Do you know how many crackers they need to eat every day? We could never afford it."

"I know. . ." said Harold sadly. "But look how cute he is. And he's made friends with Sulu, too. Can't we keep him for just one night?"

"Well, all right," said George. "But we're taking him back tomorrow."

CHAPTER 31

TOMORROW

The next day, George, Harold and Sulu returned to school with Crackers tucked snugly into Harold's book bag. Together, the four friends sneaked back upstairs to the library, where the Purple Potty stood before them in all its forbidden glory.

"Come on," said George. "Let's give this baby another spin."

"I don't know," said Harold. "Maybe we should give it a day to cool off."

"Nah, I'm sure it can be used two days in a row," said George. "What could possibly go wrong?"

"But didn't Melvin warn us not to use this machine two days in a row?" asked Harold.

"Yeah," said George. "Back in chapter 12, starting with the first word in the third line of the second paragraph on page 77."

"What exactly did he say?" asked Harold.

"Beats me," said George. "I'm not very good at remembering details."

"Well, I don't know about this," said Harold. "What if our journey brings about the end of the world as we know it?"

"That's ridiculous," said George. "It all sounds like a set-up for the sequel to a really lame children's book!"

The four friends stepped inside the Purple
Potty and closed the door behind them.
George set the controller to return them to
the Cretaceous period of the Mesozoic era
and then pulled the chain.

Suddenly, an orange light began flashing
wildly.

"Hey! I don't remember seeing an orange
light before," said Harold.

Then the Purple Potty began to shake
and rock violently.

"I don't remember this thing shaking
and rocking before, either," said George.

"Something is wrong!" cried Harold.
"Something is terribly, *terribly* wrong!"

Suddenly, the entire room lit up with an explosive burst of lightning, and the Purple Potty began to disappear into a whirlwind of electric air.

The only thing that could be heard above the chaotic clatter was the sound of two terrified voices screaming into the unknown abyss.

"Oh, NO!" screamed one of the voices.
"HERE WE GO AGAIN!" screamed
the other.

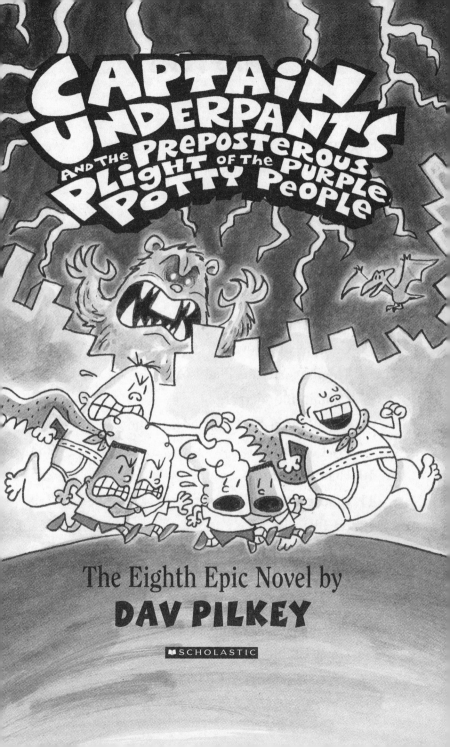

The Eighth Epic Novel by
DAV PILKEY

SCHOLASTIC

CHAPTERS

Hi everybody. As you can see, we've been experiencing some technical difficulties.
This comic book should get you up-to-date on our story so far. . .

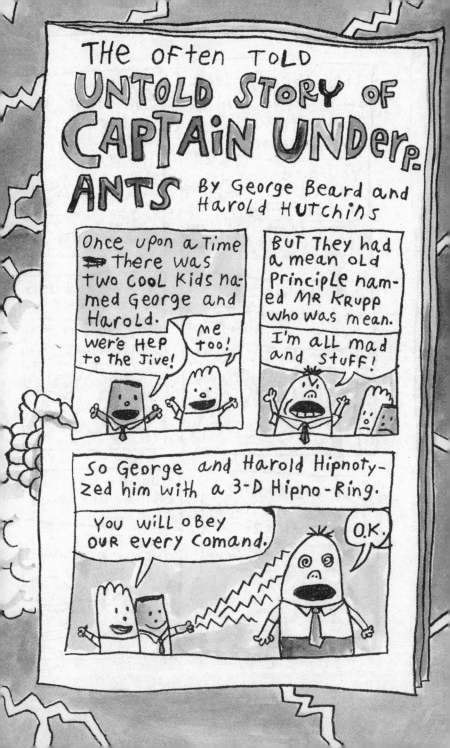

then they Axident-elly made him think He was a Super Hero.
You are captain underpants
O.K.
Look at me, I'm Captain underpants!
HA HA HA HA
But He exscaped and ran off to Fight crime.
TRA-LA-LAAA
RaTS.
George and Harold ran after him.
Hey come Back Hear
No way!
Then one day He drank some super Power Juice.
glug glug glug
Super Power Juice
Now He Has super powers and stuff.
Lookit me. I got super powers and stuff.
AW man!

In Thier Last advenchure, George and Harold got Two New pets...
a Bionic Hamster named "SULU"...
COOL!
and a pterodactyL named "Crackers"!
awesome!
EveryThing was CooL until This Brainiac Named Melv-in Showed up.
Im Telling
MeLvin made a Time machine OUT OF a PURPLE POTTY
PURPLE POTTY CO.
it Looks Like This.

CHAPTER 1

GEORGE AND HAROLD

This is George Beard and Harold Hutchins.
George is the skeleton on the right with the
tie and the flat-top. Harold is the one on
the left with the T-shirt and the bad haircut.
Remember that now.

As you might remember from our last adventure, George and Harold had recently made the horrifying mistake of trying to pass through a synthetic time warp without letting the C-2X906 super-bimflimanatrix drive of their beebleflux-capacitating zossifyer cool down, thus creating a sub-paradoxical, dimensionalistic alternicon-shift, which opened up a hyper-googliphonic screen door into a sub-omnivating ultra-zinticular bio-nanzonoflanamarzipan.

To put it in scientific terms, *they screwed up*.

But don't get all freaked out because everybody looks like a skeleton. X-ray beams are a normal by-product of inter-dimensional reality shifting. Don't worry, it'll probably clear up by the time you turn the page. . . .

See? What did I tell you?

George, Harold and their loyal pets suddenly found themselves wishing that they had never set foot inside the petrifying Purple Potty that was about to send them all on a journey into the horrifying abyss of the unknown . . . a journey that would probably spell impending doom for themselves, and would most likely bring about the end of our civilization as we know it. . .

But before I can tell you that story, I have to tell you *this* story.

CHAPTER 2

THOSE WACKY GROWN-UPS

It's been said that adults spend the first two years of their children's lives trying to make them walk and talk . . .

. . . and the next sixteen years trying to get them to sit down and shut up.

It's the same with potty training:
Most adults spend the first few years of a
child's life cheerfully discussing pee and
poopies, and how important it is to learn to
put your pee-pee and poo-poo in the potty like
big people do.

But once children have mastered the
art of toilet training, they are immediately
forbidden to ever talk about poop, pee,
toilets and other lavatory-related subjects
again. Such things are suddenly considered
rude and vulgar, and are no longer rewarded
with praise and cookies and juice boxes.

One day you're a superstar because you pooped in the toilet like a big boy, and the next day you're sitting in the principal's office because you said the word "poopy" in a history lesson (which, if you ask me, is the perfect place to say that word).

PrinciPal's
office

You're probably wondering, "Why would adults do that? Why would they encourage something one day and *discourage* it the next?"

The only answer I can think of is that adults are totally *bonkers* and should probably be avoided at all times. Perhaps you'll be lucky and find a small handful of grown-ups whom you can trust, but I'm sure we can all agree that you really have to keep an eye on most adults, most of the time.

Which is just what George and Harold did.

CHAPTER 3

THE SCHOOL OF HARD KNOCKS

Unfortunately, the adults at George and Harold's school were anything *BUT* trustworthy.

Take their principal, Mr Krupp, for example. Mr Krupp's wicked heart thrived on the teardrops of children. His very soul danced at the thought of crushing a child's spirit and dashing his or her hopes and dreams against the jagged rocks of never-ending despair.

Each day, Mr Krupp would stand at
the doorway to his office, gleefully handing
out detention slips to any child who was
unfortunate enough to cross his putrid
path — and for very minor infractions, too,
such as "smiling", "breathing without
permission", or "smelling funny".

As bad as Mr Krupp was, most of the teachers in George and Harold's school were even *worse*.

Fortunately for George and Harold, their evil educators were not very intelligent. They could be outsmarted easily, and they often were.

Now you might think that it wasn't very "sporting" of George and Harold to try and outsmart stupid people, and perhaps you'd be right. But George and Harold were just trying to make the best of a bad situation.

But unfortunately for George and Harold, their bad situation was about to get much, much worse. . .

CHAPTER 4

PURPLE POTTYVILLE

After several intense minutes of orange flashing lights, X-ray beams and lightning-infused electric whirlwinds, the Purple Potty finally stopped shaking and sputtering, and came to a sudden halt. Thick yellow smoke poured from its glowing-hot tailpipes as the grinding gears and coughing motor shifted into power-down mode.

George and Harold had no idea what to expect.

They were supposed to be perched high up in a prehistoric tree, 65 million years ago, in the Cretaceous period of the Mesozoic era. But as they stepped out the plastic door of the Purple Potty, the boys were disheartened to find themselves in the middle of the school library, exactly where they had started.

"What are we doing *here*?" asked Harold.

"I don't know," said George. "Something must have gone wrong."

Harold carefully tucked Crackers back into his book bag, and the two boys looked around the brightly-lit library.

"Well, hello, boys," said the school librarian. "This is Banned Books Week. Would you like to expand your minds today?"

"Ummm . . . no thanks," said George.

"Hey," said Harold, "didn't you get fired in our last book?"

"I don't think so," said the librarian.

"Hmmmm," said George. "I'm not feeling very good about this."

"Duh, not feeling good?" asked Melvin Sneedly, who had been struggling to comprehend the easy-to-read children's best-seller, *FrankenFart vs. the Bionic Barf Bunnies from Diarrhoea Land*. "Maybe you should go see the school nurse!"

"We have a school nurse?" asked George.

"I thought we just had a box of plasters and a rusty saw," said Harold.

"Duh, of course we have a school nurse," said Melvin. "His office is right next to our five-star gourmet cafeteria."

George and Harold looked confused.

"Uh, *thanks*," said George, "but we'll be OK."

CHAPTER 5

STRANGERS IN PARADISE LOST

As George and Harold walked down the hallway of their school, they noticed that something seemed wrong. Very wrong. But they couldn't figure out what it was.

Miss Anthrope, the unbelievably crabby school secretary, passed by the boys and smiled kindly.

"Why, hello, George and Harold," she said. "It's so good to see you two. Have a wonderful day!"

George and Harold looked at her suspiciously.

"Ummmm . . . *what just happened*?" asked Harold.

"I don't know," said George. "But something strange sure is going on."

George and Harold opened their locker
and carefully put Crackers and Sulu inside.

"Shhhh. . . They're asleep," said George.

"Good," said Harold. "They can take a
nap while we get to class."

211

On the way to their classroom, George and Harold stopped to switch the letters around on the lunch menu sign.

But just as they were finishing, their principal, Mr Krupp, caught them red-handed.

"Hey, bubs!" he said. "What are you kids
doing out here?"

"Uh . . . ummm. . ." George stammered.
"Y'see, we were ummm. . ."

"*Please eat my plump, juicy boogers?*"
said Mr Krupp, giggling with glee. "That's
gotta be the funniest thing I've seen all
day! You boys really crack me up! You're
hilarious!" Then, with a spring in his step,
Mr Krupp pranced away, whistling a
merry tune.

"Ummmm . . . *what just happened*?" asked Harold.

"Shhhh!" whispered George. "Look!"

George pointed at two kids who were coming towards them, reading a home-made comic book. The kid on the left had a T-shirt and a flat-top. The one on the right had a tie and a bad haircut. Please feel free to remember that now, if you wish.

"It's – it's *US*!" whispered George.

"How can they be us?" whispered Harold. "I thought *we* were us!"

PLEASE EAT
MY PLUMP,
JUICY
BOOGER

George and Harold hid behind a rubbish bin as their two look-alikes walked towards them. They stopped in front of the lunch menu sign and frowned. Then a devilish look came over their faces as they quickly began rearranging the letters.

The strange boys snickered wickedly as they sneaked away from their prank.

"Ummmm . . . *what just happened*?" asked Harold.

"I think I've figured it out," said George.

CHAPTER 6

THE WORLD ACCORDING TO GEORGE

"I think the Purple Potty brought us to some kind of strange, backwards universe," said George.

"No way," said Harold. "That kind of thing only happens in poorly written children's stories whose authors have clearly begun running out of ideas!"

"Here, I'll prove it," said George.

The two friends walked to the cafeteria and took a whiff.

"That's weird," said Harold. "It doesn't smell like dirty nappies, greasy dishwater and mouldy tennis shoes in here any more. It smells like – like *food*!"

"Yep," said George.

Next, the boys went to the gymnasium.

"That's weird," said Harold. "Our gym teacher isn't fat any more. And he's not being incredibly cruel to the non-athletic kids like he usually is."

"Yep," said George.

Finally, George and Harold stepped outside.

"That's weird," said Harold. "All of our evilest and most terrifying enemies from the past have been miraculously transformed into good guys."

"Yep," said George.

CHAPTER 7

GETTIN' OUTTA TOWN

George and Harold ran back to their locker.

"Let's grab Crackers and Sulu and get out of this crazy place," said George.

"Good idea," said Harold.

But when they opened the locker door,
their two friends were missing.

"*Where the heck are Crackers and Sulu?*"
cried George.

"I dunno. . ." said Harold. "Nobody else
has the combination to our locker. Nobody
else except. . ."

". . .*our twins!*" gasped George.

Harold tried to shut their locker, but the door jammed on something.

"What's that?" asked George.

"Looks like a comic book," said Harold. He held it up and read the front cover out loud. At that moment, George and Harold began to get a dreadful sense of the horror they were up against.

CHAPTER 9

NOT WITHOUT MY HAMSTER (. . . AND MY PTERODACTYL)

"I think our evil twins made this comic book," said Harold.

"They must have," said George. "The artwork is really bad, and I'm pretty sure they misspelled some words."

"Let's get out of here," said Harold.

"Not without Crackers and Sulu," said George.

George and Harold ran to a window and looked out. There they saw their two evil twins sneaking home, carrying their beloved pets with them.

"Sulu and Crackers have no idea what's going on," said George. "They think those two guys are US!"

"How in the world are we going to stop US?" asked Harold.

CHAPTER 10
HYPNO-HORROR

George and Harold knew exactly where those evil twins had taken Crackers and Sulu. To the same place *they* would have taken them: their tree house.

So our two heroes dashed home as fast as they could. Then they climbed up the tree house ladder as *quietly* as they could.

But when they peeked inside, they saw
something that was three hundred and
eighty-nine times worse than they ever could have
imagined. Their evil twins were
hypnotizing their beloved pets with a 3-D
Hypno-Ring.

"You will obey our every command," said
Evil Harold.

"Yeah," said Evil George. "And you'll be
really wicked from now on, too!"

George and Harold gasped, which is actually not
a very smart thing to do if you're trying
to go unnoticed.

"Hey, *LOOK*!" shouted Evil Harold. "*GASPERS!*"

"GET 'EM!" shouted Evil George to their newly hypnotized pets.

Crackers didn't move. The dazed pterodactyl shook his head and looked a little confused. But Sulu immediately sprung into action. He lunged at George and Harold, grabbed them by their shirts, and yanked them to the ground.

"Hey!" said Evil George. "Those kids look
just like us. What should we do with them?"

"We can't take any chances," said Evil
Harold. Then he called to Sulu in a loud
and commanding voice, "DESTROY THEM,
O WICKED HAMSTER!"

CHAPTER 11
CRACKERS TO THE RESCUE

Crackers did not understand what was going on, but the plucky pterodactyl knew that something needed to be done . . . and *quickly*. So with a sudden whoosh of flapping wings, Crackers swooped in and grabbed George and Harold from the relentless little paws of their raging robotic rodent rival.

"Oh, NO!" screamed Harold. "Crackers is going to fly us high into the air and drop us! We're DOOMED!"

"Actually, I think *he's* trying to *rescue* us," said George.

"But *he* got hypnotized just like Sulu," said Harold. "Why on Earth would *he* do the opposite of what *he* was ordered to do?"

"And how come all of our pronouns are getting italicized?" asked George.

"Let's not worry about that now," said Harold. "We've gotta get out of here!"

"But we can't leave Sulu behind," cried George.

"Don't worry," said Harold. "We'll come back for Sulu!"

So the three friends flew to the school and headed upstairs to the library.

"Hey! That looks like a pterodactyl," said Mr Krupp as our heroes pushed past him. "Let me stroke him! Let me stroke him!" Mr Krupp cried, chasing after them.

George, Harold and Crackers finally reached the library just in time to see Sulu and their evil twins smash through the ceiling with a terrible crash.

"You jerks won't get away from us *THIS* time," said Evil Harold.

Desperately, George, Harold and Crackers tumbled into the Purple Potty, slammed the door shut, and quickly reset the controls.

Mr Krupp and Sulu pounded on the door of the Purple Potty, while George and Harold's evil twins shook the malfunctioning time machine from side to side.

All at once, an orange light started flashing wildly. The Purple Potty began to shake and wobble violently. Then the entire room lit up with an explosive burst of lightning as the Purple Potty (and everyone around it) disappeared into a whirlwind of electric air.

CHAPTER 12

KA-BLAMSKI!

Suddenly, there was another blinding flash
of light. Everyone around the Purple Potty
flew off in different directions. Then the
Purple Potty stopped shaking and wobbling,
and switched into shut-down mode.

READING
MIGHT
OFFEND
YOU

...WHY TAKE
A CHANCE?

George, Harold and Crackers peeked out.

"Look," said Harold. "There aren't any books in this library. We must be back in our own reality."

"But we've got to be sure," said George.

The two boys tucked Crackers into Harold's book bag and crept out into the hallway. As they peered into the windows of nearby classrooms, they saw room after room of heartbroken and despondent-looking children.

Some were standing in corners, weeping . . . others were sitting on dunce stools wearing humiliating hats . . . while still others were writing unbelievably degrading sentences over and over on the chalkboard as their teachers rifled through their lunch boxes, stealing all of the best desserts.

"Yep," sighed George, "we're back in our own reality."

"I never thought I'd say this," said Harold, "but it's good to be home."

"*To the tree house!*" cried George.

CHAPTER 13

PURPLE POTTY PEOPLE UNITE!

Seconds after George, Harold and Crackers left the library, four confused beings from an alternative dimension began to stir. Evil George, Evil Harold, Evil Sulu and Nice Mr Krupp stumbled to the centre of the strange, empty library, rubbing their heads and looking around curiously.

"Look," said Evil George. "This library has no books on the shelves."

"Hmmmm," said Evil Harold. "It looks like we've entered some kind of alternative universe. An illogical reality where everything is backwards."

"Backwards, eh?" said Evil George. "*WE* could do quite well in a place like this!"

He walked over to the drinking fountain and splashed some water on Nice Mr Krupp's face.

Suddenly, Nice Mr Krupp's confused
smile turned into an evil frown. He ripped
off his clothes and tied a curtain from a
nearby window around his neck. Then Evil
George handed him a bad toupee, and the
pernicious principal stood before them,
snarling angrily through his flared nostrils.

"I AM CAPTAIN BLUNDERPANTS!" he
shouted in a thunderous voice.

CHAPTER 14

THE CHAPTER WHERE SOME STUFF HAPPENS

Meanwhile, back at their tree house, George and Harold grabbed some supplies before heading off to save Sulu.

"We'll need our 3-D Hypno-Ring," said George, "to change Sulu back to his old self again."

"Cool!" said Harold. "And we'd better take the rest of this Extra-Strength Super Power Juice, just in case."

"Good idea," said George.

The two friends stuffed their supplies and their pet pterodactyl into their book bags and headed down the tree house ladder.

"*Just where the heck do you two think you're going?*" asked a commanding voice at the bottom of the ladder. It was George's dad, and he didn't seem very happy.

"Uh," said George, "we-we need to go back to school for something."

"Yeah," said Harold. "We forgot something."

"Well, it'll have to wait until tomorrow," said George's dad. "We're having dinner with the Hutchinses tonight, remember?"

"Oh yeah," said George. "It's Grandparents' Day. We almost forgot."

"Well, you're just in time for dinner," said George's dad. "Go inside and wash your hands."

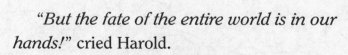

"*But the fate of the entire world is in our hands!*" cried Harold.

"The fate of the entire world can wait until tomorrow," said George's dad.

CHAPTER 15
SUPER SUPPER

After they'd washed their hands, the two boys went to the dining room. George's parents had prepared a big meal, and everybody waited patiently for George and Harold to join them. Harold's mum, sister and grandpa were there, along with George's mum, dad and his great-grandma.

"Hello, babies," said George's great-grandma. "What have you boys been up to today?"

"Nothin'," said George as he hugged his great-grandma.

"We made you and Grandpa a comic book yesterday," said Harold.

"Did you?" said Harold's grandpa. "Well, let's have a look!"

George shuffled through his book bag, taking things out and laying them on the table. "It's here somewhere," he said. Finally, he pulled out two copies of their latest comic book, "The Adventures of Boxer Boy and Great-Granny Girdle".

"It's about how you guys turn into
superheroes and save the world and stuff,"
said George.

"I drew the pictures," said Harold.

"Well, that's very nice, boys," said
George's dad. "Now sit down, and let's eat."

"We *can't*!" said George. "We've got to go now. It's really important!"

George and Harold's grandparents poured themselves a glass of juice and began reading their new comic books, while the boys continued arguing with George's dad.

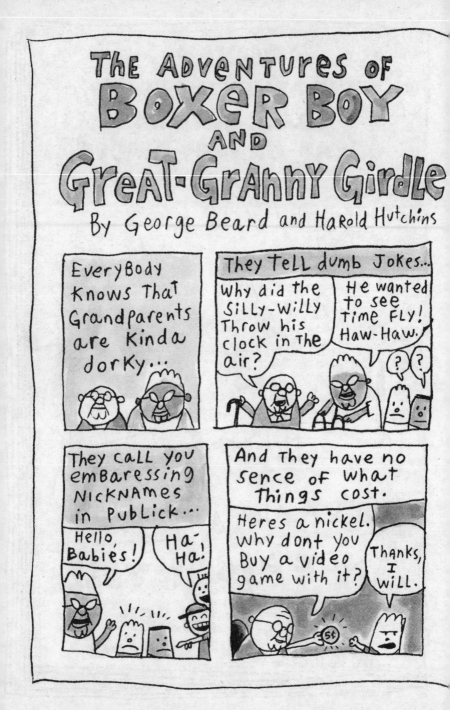

LATER
Mmm. Those candys were good. I feeL so strong!
Me To! I Feel Power-FULL
OH No!!! Those guys ate all my super Power Hard cAndy!
uh, oh
HARd CANDY
George and Harolds Grandparents Joined hands....
Geezer Powers ACTiVATe!!
and They spin-ed around and around.....
Soon They were Transformed!
Im BOXER BoY!
Im Great-Granny Girdle
Im out of here!
Im with you!

The RoBo-Geezers attacked. But Boxer Boy and Great Granny Girdle were...
Faster than a speding electric scooter...
ZOOM
More powerful than adult diapers...
BONK
Diapers
Wet 'em and Forget 'em
and able to Leap Tall buildings without Breaking a hip!!!
weeeee

BUT...
There's too many of Them!
I have a idea. Let Them chase you For a while.
So The RoBoTS all Chased Great Granny GirdLe...
and Boxer Boy attacked the space Ship.
HEY!
POW
PUNCH
BAM
BANG
CRASH

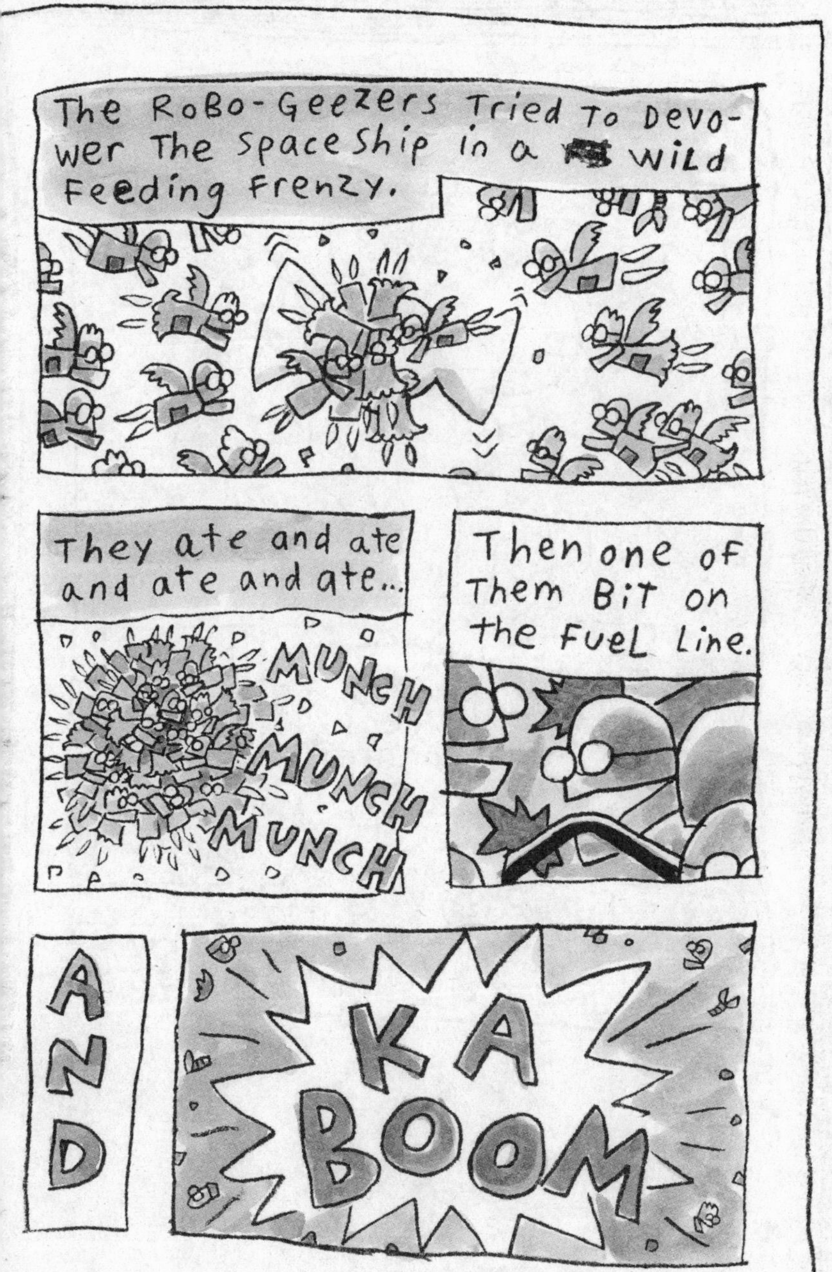

CHAPTER 17

MEANWHILE, BACK AT THE TREE HOUSE. . .

While George and Harold pleaded with George's dad to be excused from dinner, a pack of evil thugs was just outside their window, sneaking up into their tree house.

"We've got to create some kind of diversion while we unleash our sinful scheme," said Evil Harold. The villains looked around the tree house for anything they could use.

"What's this little thing?" said Evil George. He pressed the button on the back of the miniature Goosy-Grow 4000. Suddenly, a beam of energy shot out of the tiny contraption, accidentally zapping Evil Sulu, who was tucked inside Evil Harold's shirt pocket.

Immediately, Evil Sulu began to grow bigger and bigger until he leaped out of Evil Harold's pocket and fell to the floor with a giant *THUD*! Evil Sulu was now the size of a fully-grown sheepdog. The villains all smiled at one another as they watched Evil Sulu growl and snarl ferociously.

"I think we've found our diversion," said
Evil George, as he zapped Evil Sulu again.

CHAPTER 18
CRASH !

Suddenly, Evil Sulu grew to the size of a giant monster. He jumped out of the tree house and landed in George's garden with a terrible, thunderous crash.

"*What was that?*" cried George's dad.

Everyone jumped up and dashed
outside to get a better look at the horrible
creature that towered over the house,
snarling and roaring hideously. For some
strange reason, George and Harold's
grandparents jumped up and dashed the
fastest—faster than they had moved in

years—but nobody really noticed because
of the giant hamster thing.

"What's going on?" cried Harold.

"Those evil guys must have followed
us back to our own reality somehow,"
whispered George. "We've gotta stop them
before they take over OUR WORLD!"

Sulu crashed and smashed his way
through the neighbourhood, heading towards
the big city . . . because, well, that's where
giant monsters usually head. George ran
inside and grabbed the 3-D Hypno-Ring and
the Super Power Juice (which felt surprisingly
empty), and whistled for Crackers. And while
the grown-ups were fussing and fretting over
trivial things like broken fences, insurance
policies and property-damage reports,
George, Harold and Crackers flew off to
save the world.

CHAPTER 19

WHENHAMSTERSATTACK.COM

Soon the three friends soared over the centre of the city. There they met up with their beloved pet, Sulu, who was now a giant, evil monster destroying everything in his path.

"Well," said Harold, "it looks like you
and I are going to have to drink that Super
Power Juice so we can stop Giant Evil Sulu
from wrecking the city."

"Uh, Harold?" said George, as he eyed the
carton of Super Power Juice suspiciously.

"I'm so *psyched*!" said Harold. "I've always
wanted to have super powers!"

"Uh . . . *Harold*?" said George again,
as he held the carton to his ear and
shook it back and forth.

"I hope I get Kung-Fu Grip . . . and X-ray vision!" said Harold. "That would be awesome!"

"Uh . . . *HAROLD*???" shouted George, as he turned the Super Power Juice carton upside down. "There's nothing left."

"*What do you mean?*" cried Harold. "There was, like, a *third* of a carton in there twenty minutes ago!"

"Well, it's gone now," said George. "It must have evaporated or something."

The boys watched helplessly as Giant Evil Sulu continued trashing the city.

"Well," said George, "I guess there's just one thing left to do."

Hurriedly, the three friends flew to the house of their principal, Mr Krupp. It was easy to find, since it was the only house on Curmudgeon Boulevard that was covered in toilet paper.

"Next time we've gotta use single-ply toilet paper," said George. "We'll get better coverage."

After a quick knock on the door, and an even quicker snap of the fingers, Mr Krupp transformed into the Amazing Captain Underpants. And in no time at all, the world's greatest, baldest superhero was face-to-face with the world's biggest, baddest bionic hamster.

CHAPTER 20

THE INCREDIBLY GRAPHIC VIOLENCE CHAPTER, PART 1 (IN FLIP-O-RAMA™)

Introducing
FLIP-O
Back in the olden days, incredibly graphic violence was believed to be harmful, dangerous, and even immoral.
But now it's fun for the whole family, thanks to the science of Flip-O-Rama!

PILKEY® BRAND
⊃·RAMA

HERE'S HOW IT WORKS!

STEP 1
First, place your *left* hand inside the dotted lines marked "LEFT HAND HERE". Hold the book open *flat*.

STEP 2
Grasp the *right-hand* page with your right thumb and index finger (inside the dotted lines marked "RIGHT THUMB HERE").

STEP 3
Now *quickly* flip the right-hand page back and forth until the picture appears to be *animated*.

(For extra fun, try adding your own sound-effects!)

FLIP-O-RAMA 1

(pages 289 and 291)

Remember, flip *only* page 289.
While you are flipping, be sure you
can see the picture on page 289
and the one on page 291.
If you flip quickly, the two
pictures will start to look like
<u>one</u> *animated* picture.

Don't forget to
add your own sound-effects!

LEFT HAND HERE

HAMSTER HAVOC

HAMSTER HAVOC

FLIP-O-RAMA 2

(pages 293 and 295)

Remember, flip *only* page 293.
While you are flipping, be sure you
can see the picture on page 293
and the one on page 295.
If you flip quickly, the two
pictures will start to look like
<u>one</u> *animated* picture.

Don't forget to
add your own sound-effects!

LEFT HAND HERE

PUT YOUR HEAD
ON MY BOULDER

293

RIGHT
THUMB
HERE

PUT YOUR HEAD
ON MY BOULDER

CHAPTER 21

THE ANTI-CLIMACTIC CHAPTER

The battle between man and beast was over. George and Harold petted Sulu's giant face and breathed a sigh of relief.

"He'll be OK," said George. "He just got knocked out."

"Great!" said Harold. "It looks like all of our problems are over!"

"NOT SO FAST!" said a voice that came from somewhere on the lower right-hand corner of the next page.

It was Evil George, along with Evil Harold and the Ultra-Evil Captain Blunderpants.

The terrible trio had been busy working on their preposterous plight (which is just a fancy way of saying that they were busy robbing a bank).

"Somebody's been messing with our giant attack hamster," said Evil Harold. "I think we need to teach those goody-goodies a lesson!"

"And I'm just the guy to do it!" said Captain Blunderpants proudly.

Instantly, the mood shifted. Everyone stood back. The air crackled with tension. The showdown of the century was about to begin. Captain Underpants would soon engage in a historic battle with his evil twin. Never before had our brave hero encountered an enemy who was so powerful. Kilogram for kilogram, super power for super power, Captain Underpants was pitted against his equal. He had met his match. It was to be the ultimate smackdown . . . an all-out war . . . the brawl to end all brawls . . . the definitive clash between good and evil . . . a momentous confrontation of the most critical —

SNAP!

George snapped his fingers, and suddenly the horrifyingly evil Captain Blunderpants transformed into a friendly elementary school principal.

"Awww, maaaaaan!" cried Evil George and Evil Harold.

"We read your comic book back in chapter 8," said Harold. "Didja think we wouldn't remember how to turn your evil super-villain back into a harmless principal?"

George and Harold quickly found some
rope and tied up Evil George, Evil Harold,
and Nice Mr Krupp. "We're taking you losers
back to your own reality where you won't
bother us ever again!" said George.

"All we have to do is de-hypnotize and
shrink Sulu, and our job will be done!" said
Harold. "Nothing can possibly go wrong now!"

"Y'know, you really shouldn't say things
like that," said George.

"Why?" said Harold.

CHAPTER 22
KA-BOOM!

Suddenly, lightning flashed, thunder crashed, and the rain came a-tumbling down.

"*That's why!*" said George.

As the first few drops of rain hit Captain Underpants's pudgy face, he began to transform. In a matter of seconds, he changed from a confident, powerful superhero into an angry, annoyed elementary school principal.

Unlikewisely, the rain-on-the-face thing was having the opposite effect on Nice Mr Krupp, transforming him, once again, into an arrogant, foul-tempered super-villain called Captain Blunderpants.

Evil George and Evil Harold smiled their evilest smiles as Captain Blunderpants snapped their ropes and yelled out a triumphant "La-La-Traaaaa!"

George and Harold quickly snapped their fingers again and again, but it was having no effect. It was raining too hard, and Mr Krupp was getting annoyed.

"This is the dumbest dream I've ever had!" he shouted. "I'm gonna go home and get back into bed." And with that, he turned and stormed off towards his soggy toilet-paper-covered house.

SNAP SNAP SNAP SNAP

"Looks like the tables have turned," Evil Harold snickered.

"You guys haven't won yet," said George. Quickly, George and Harold leaped on to Crackers's back, and the three forlorn friends flew off towards their tree house.

"Don't just stand there!" cried Evil Harold to his creepy cohorts. "LET'S GET 'EM!"

CHAPTER 23

TWO MINUTES LATER. . .

Back in George's yard, our heroes searched furiously through their tree house.

"I found it!" cried George. "The Shrinky-Pig 2000! All we have to do is shrink those evil losers, and we'll save the world!"

"*Too late!*" shouted Captain Blunderpants as he grabbed George and Harold by their shirt collars.

"We'll take that 'Shrinky-Thingy'," said Evil Harold, as the contraption slipped out of George's arms. "I'm not sure how it works, but once I figure it out, I can think of about *a million and nine* evil things to do with it!"

Captain Blunderpants held George and Harold high in the air and snarled viciously.

"Prepare to be PULVERIZED!" he shouted.

"We're *DOOMED!*" screamed Harold.

"NOW WAIT JUST A COTTON-PICKIN' MINUTE, YOUNG FELLA!" shouted a familiar-sounding voice from inside George's house. . .

CHAPTER 24

NOBODY MESSES WITH OUR GRANDBABIES!

Harold's grandpa and George's great-grandma stepped out on to the back patio and confronted the big bully, Captain Blunderpants.

"You put those babies down or you'll get the whuppin' of your lifetime," said George's great-grandma.

Captain Blunderpants laughed haughtily.

"We're not going to warn you again, Skippy," said Harold's grandpa.

Captain Blunderpants continued to tighten his grip on George and Harold.

So the two octogenarians joined hands, gazed fiercely into each other's eyes, and shouted, "Geezer Powers *ACTIVATE*!"

Quickly they began spinning around and around. Faster and faster the old folks twirled until a tornado formed around them, tearing away their clothes and jewellery, and sending patio furniture flying violently.

Suddenly, the twirling stopped, the tornado subsided, and the elderly twosome stood proudly in their underwear, huffing, puffing, and fearlessly facing their foe.

"Oooh, that was fun. Let's do it again, Henry," said George's great-grandma.

"Heh-heh," laughed Harold's grandpa. "All right, my dear, but we've gotta teach that fat boy a lesson first."

"Oh yeah," said George's great-grandma. "That young fella's got a hankerin' for a spankerin'!"

Harold's grandpa grabbed a couple of curtains from the kitchen window and tied them around their necks. "Not too tight, Henry," said George's great-grandma.

With their capes in place, George and Harold's super-grandparents approached Captain Blunderpants triumphantly.

"All right, sonny," said Harold's grandpa. "Prepare to get your bucket whupped by Boxer Boy and Great-Granny Girdle!"

CHAPTER 25

THE INCREDIBLY GRAPHIC VIOLENCE CHAPTER, PART 2 (IN FLIP-O-RAMA™)

FLIP-O-RAMA 3

(pages 317 and 319)

Remember, flip *only* page 317.
While you are flipping, be sure you
can see the picture on page 317
and the one on page 319.
If you flip quickly, the two
pictures will start to look like
<u>one</u> *animated* picture.

Don't forget to
add your own sound-effects!

LEFT HAND HERE

THE GERIATRIC
JAWBREAKER

RIGHT
THUMB
HERE

THE GERIATRIC
JAWBREAKER

FLIP-O-RAMA 4

(pages 321 and 323)

Remember, flip *only* page 321.
While you are flipping, be sure you
can see the picture on page 321
and the one on page 323.
If you flip quickly, the two
pictures will start to look like
<u>one</u> *animated* picture.

Don't forget to
add your own sound-effects!

LEFT HAND HERE

A CANE
IN THE BRAIN

321

RIGHT
THUMB
HERE

A CANE
IN THE BRAIN

FLIP-O-RAMA 5

(pages 325 and 327)

Remember, flip *only* page 325.
While you are flipping, be sure you
can see the picture on page 325
and the one on page 327.
If you flip quickly, the two
pictures will start to look like
<u>one</u> *animated* picture.

Don't forget to
add your own sound-effects!

LEFT HAND HERE

TAKE A WALKER
ON THE WILD SIDE

325

RIGHT
THUMB
HERE

RIGHT
INDEX
FINGER
HERE

TAKE A WALKER ON THE WILD SIDE

CHAPTER 26
SHRINKY-DORKS

"Y'know," said George, "I think I just figured out what happened to the Super Power Juice that disappeared earlier."

"Oh yeah?" said Evil George. "But you didn't figure *THIS* out! All we have to do is press ONE BUTTON on this shrinking machine, and you'll all be transformed into tiny little shrimps!"

"Go ahead and press the button!" laughed Harold. "You're holding it backwards anyway. You'll just shrink yourselves!"

"Really?" said Evil Harold. "Gee, thanks!" He turned the Shrinky-Pig 2000 around and pressed the button.

And they were shrunk to the size of potato chips.

"Hey!" shouted Mini Evil George. "What happened?"

"Oops," said Harold. "I guess I made a mistake. You actually *WERE* holding it right the first time."

"Y'know," said George, "I think I know two little boys who could really use a good spanking!"

CHAPTER 27

THE INCREDIBLY GRAPHIC VIOLENCE CHAPTER, PART 3 (IN FLIP-O-RAMA™)

LEFT HAND HERE

HAPPY
SPANKSGIVING

RIGHT
THUMB
HERE

HAPPY
SPANKSGIVING

CHAPTER 28

WRAPPING THINGS UP

"Well, it looks like our job here is done," said Boxer Boy.

"Yes, it is, my big strong man," said Great-Granny Girdle, giggling gleefully.

George and Harold looked at each other in horror.

"Y'know, little lady," said Boxer Boy, "somewhere out there is an all-you-can-eat buffet with a *Senior Citizens' Early-Bird Special* just going to waste!"

"Well, let's go find
it, you big hunk-o-love!"
said Great-Granny Girdle as she kissed
him passionately on his wobbly neck fat.

The scene that followed could best be
described as the drooliest five-minute kiss
in the history of children's books. Dentures
sloshed, wrinkles flapped, and rubbery
jowls squished, smooshed and quivered
gelatinously.

"Ummm," said Harold, "I think I need to
go wash my eyeballs."

"Me, too," said George.

And as the Arthritic Avengers flew off into the sunset, George and Harold decided to try very, VERY hard not to think about the disgusting event they had just witnessed.

"C'mon, we've gotta wrap this story up," said George. "First we need to de-hypnotize and shrink Sulu."

"Then we've gotta go back into that crazy Purple Potty and return these bozos to their alternative universe," said Harold.

338

CHAPTER 29

TO MAKE A LONG STORY SHORT

ZAP!

CHAPTER 30

TO MAKE A LONGER STORY EVEN SHORTER

KICK!

CHAPTER 31

THE CHAPTER WHERE NOTHING BAD HAPPENS

"Gee, that worked out pretty good," said Harold. "Sulu is now back to his normal size and personality, and the Purple Potty People are back in their own reality where they won't be able to bother us ever again. I guess everything worked out perfectly!"

"Yeah, *nice going*," said George, looking a bit annoyed. "Why do you have to say things like that?"

"Things like *what*?" asked Harold.

"Haven't you been paying attention in these stories?" asked George. "Every time somebody says something like that, it always means that a buncha bad stuff is just about to happen."

"But what could possibly go wrong now?" asked Harold.

"*FREEZE!*" shouted the Chief of Police. "You guys are under arrest for robbing Frank's Bank. Looks like you're going to jail for the rest of your lives!"

"See what I mean?" said George. "You've gotta stop saying stuff like that!"

"I guess you're right," said Harold. "But at least things can't get any worse."

"Aaaaugh!" shouted George. "You did it *again*! Now I bet when you turn the page, something even *worse* is going to happen! You've gotta learn to keep your mouth shut at the end of these books!"

"Yeah, but what could be worse than going to jail for the rest of our lives?"

CHAPTER 32

THE THING THAT COULD BE WORSE THAN GOING TO JAIL FOR THE REST OF THEIR LIVES

Suddenly, out of nowhere, a ball of blue lightning appeared, growing bigger and bigger, until it exploded in a blinding flash.

And there, standing where the ball of lightning had been, was a smoking pair of giant robotic trousers.

"This can't be good," said George.

A small opening at the front of the robo-
trousers began to unzip. And out of that
opening peeked a fearsomely familiar face.

"Hey! It's Professor Poopypants!" shouted
Harold.

The cops started to laugh.

"Stop LAUGHING!" shouted the little man
peeking out of the giant zipper. "My name is
no longer Professor Poopypants. I changed it
to Tippy Tinkletrousers!"

The cops laughed even harder.

"And I've got a *special surprise* for anybody who thinks my NEW name is funny!" said the furious professor.

Immediately, the metallic trousers opened up at the top, and a giant laser shooter rose from its robotic depths.

346

A brilliant burst of energy zapped the laughing cops, and suddenly they were both transformed into frozen statues.

"My Freezy-Beam 4000 will take care of anybody who stands in my way!" said Tippy. "And now," he said with a wicked smile, "it's time for my *revenge*!"

"OH, NO!" screamed George.
"HERE WE GO AGAIN!" screamed Harold.

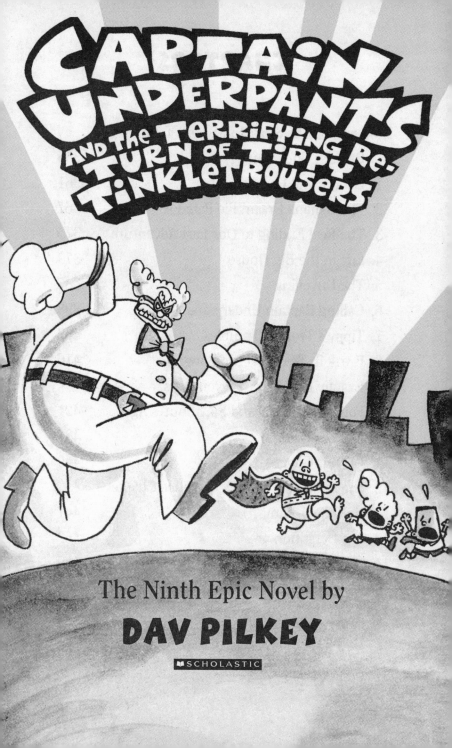

CHAPTERS

Hi everybody. The last time you saw us, we were headed to jail for the rest of our lives. Then something even WORSE happened.
Check out this comic book to get caught up on our story so far!

CHAPTER 1
GEORGE AND HAROLD

This is George Beard and Harold Hutchins.
George is the kid on the right with the tie
and the flat-top. Harold is the one on the
left with the T-shirt and the bad haircut.
Remember that now.

When our last adventure ended, George and Harold were being escorted to jail. The police had discovered surveillance photos showing the two boys robbing a bank with Captain Underpants. Of course, we all know that George, Harold and Captain Underpants were innocent. It was their *evil twins* who had robbed that bank. But the police hadn't bothered to read the last book, so they really didn't know what was going on.

All they knew was that George and Harold *looked* a lot like the two kids in the surveillance photos. So the cops yelled *"FREEZE!"* and grabbed George and Harold, then told the two boys of their terrible fate.

Suddenly, a gigantic pair of robotic trousers appeared from out of nowhere. The terrifying Tippy Tinkletrousers emerged from the zipper, zapped the cops with an ice ray. . .

. . .and chased George and Harold (and their
two pets, Crackers and Sulu) far into the
cavernous depths of the lower right-hand
corner of page 365.

If you read our last epic novel, you know
that this is how the story ended. But that's
not how it was *supposed* to end.

You see, Tippy and his giant ice-ray-zapping robotic trousers weren't supposed to be there at all. They had come from the future and rudely interrupted what was *supposed* to happen.

Unfortunately for Tippy, the simple act of sending himself backwards through time would end up being a terrible, terrible mistake. A mistake that would ultimately lead to the destruction of our entire planet, more or less.

But before I can tell you that story, I have to tell you *this* story. . .

CHAPTER 2

THE BANANA CREAM PIE PARADOX

Time machines are awesome. There's no doubt about it. But they can also be very dangerous. It's possible that a person could go back in time and accidentally change one little thing – and that one teeny, tiny, itsy-bitsy thing could profoundly affect the future. This is what scientists refer to as the *Banana Cream Pie Paradox*.

THE BANANA CREAM PIE PARADOX

PLEASE FOLLOW ALONG
WITH THESE HANDY ILLUSTRATIONS:

Imagine, if you will, that a scientist from the year 2020 baked a banana cream pie using bananas that he harvested from his very own banana tree.

Let's suppose now that this scientist took his banana cream pie into a time machine, which zapped him (and the pie) back to the year 1936.

Now imagine that the scientist stepped out of his time machine and accidentally tripped, smashing his pie into the face of a lady sitting at a fancy garden party.

Now suppose that the lady jumped up
angrily, wiped a handful of gooey
banana cream pie filling from
her face, and threw it
at the scientist.

The scientist ducked. . .

. . .causing the banana goo to smack into
the face of a gentleman standing nearby.

A waitress pointed
at the gentleman
and laughed.

The angry gentleman
wiped the goo from
his face. . .

. . . and smooshed it into
the waitress's face.

SMOOSH!

"Well!" said the waitress. "I've never been so insulted in all my life!"

"You oughtta get out more, lady! N'yuk, n'yuk, n'yuk!" said a chubby bald guy.

"Why don't you mind your own business, birdbrain?" said another man. . .

. . .as he poked
the chubby
bald guy in
the eyes.

The tiny banana tree snapped
in half and died.

Now, if the scientist's banana tree died in 1936, it could never grow up and produce bananas.

Therefore, the scientist would not have had the main ingredient he used to make his banana cream pie in the year 2020.

Consequently, the banana cream pie could not exist.

TELL THAT TO
THESE GUYS!

Many scientists throughout the centuries have pondered the Banana Cream Pie Paradox and have come to the conclusion that people should be really, really, really, REALLY, *REALLY* careful when they use time machines. Because one simple change in the past could affect the future . . . and even possibly destroy our entire planet.

CHAPTER 3

THE REAL ENDING TO OUR LAST ADVENTURE

As we already saw in Chapter 1, George and Harold were being taken to jail when Tippy Tinkletrousers travelled backwards through time and interfered. But what would have happened if he hadn't showed up? What was *supposed* to happen (before Tippy so rudely interrupted them)? Well, sit back and get comfortable, because you're about to find out!

The Police Chief and his right-hand man, Officer McWiggly, handcuffed George and Harold and shuffled them into the back of their police car.

"You've got the wrong guys," cried Harold. "We didn't rob that bank!"

"It's true," said George. "That bank was robbed by our evil twins from an alternate universe!"

"Yeah, *right*," said Officer McWiggly. "If I had a penny for every time I've heard *THAT* excuse!"

On the way to jail, the cops drove past Mr
Krupp, who was busy cleaning up the soggy
toilet paper in his yard.

"Hey!" shouted the Police Chief. "That's
the guy who robbed the bank with those kids!"

"Let's get him!" yelled Officer McWiggly.

The cops slammed on the brakes, grabbed Mr Krupp, handcuffed him, and threw him into the backseat of the car along with George and Harold.

Their trials lasted for nearly a year, and George, Harold, and Mr Krupp were all found guilty. They were each sentenced to ten years of incarceration. This unusually harsh sentence was tough on George and Harold, but it was *REALLY* hard on Mr Krupp!

CHAPTER 4

LIFE IN THE BIG HOUSE

Poor Mr Krupp. He had been locked up at the Piqua State Penitentiary for months, and the life of a jailbird just wasn't his thing. All day long he had people bossing him around. He ate nutritionally deficient, horrible-tasting meals in a filthy cafeteria. He got bullied constantly by a bunch of meat-headed thugs and he spent his days doing menial "busy work" in an overcrowded, poorly ventilated sweatshop.

Mr Krupp was told when to eat, when to read, and when to exercise. He even had to ask permission to go to the bathroom! He was constantly bombarded with pointless rules, ridiculous discipline, random searches, metal detectors, security cameras, and pharmaceuticals designed to make everyone compliant and docile. It was a lot like being a student at Jerome Horwitz Elementary School, except that the prison had better funding.

Mr Krupp grumbled angrily to himself as he stomped around the prison courtyard on a gloomy autumn afternoon. In the centre of the courtyard, a giant green tarp shielded everyone's eyes from something large and tall that was being built in honour of the Piqua State Penitentiary's upcoming ten-year anniversary. Everyone assumed it was some kind of statue, but since nobody had seen this top-secret project (not even the warden), nobody was quite sure *what* it was.

"I'm sick of this place," Mr Krupp muttered to himself. "Everybody's always telling me what to do! If *ONE MORE PERSON* gives me another order, I think I'm going to go *CRAZY*!"

"Hey, fatty!" shouted a tiny inmate working behind the green tarp. "Gimme that hammer over there!"

Mr Krupp clenched his fists furiously. "YOU CAN'T TELL ME WHAT TO DO!" he screamed. "YOU'RE A PRISONER JUST LIKE I AM!"

"I most certainly am *nothing* like you," said the tiny prisoner. It was Tippy Tinkletrousers, who was serving an eight- year sentence for attempting to take over the planet with intent to enslave humanity.

Mr Krupp rolled up his sweaty sleeves and stomped over to the pint-sized prisoner.

He eyed Tippy up and down. Tippy eyed Mr Krupp down and up.

"Hey!" Mr Krupp shouted. "You look kinda familiar!"

"I agree!" said Tippy. "But I can't quite remember where I've seen you before!"

The two men walked in slow circles around each other.

"Well, whoever you are," Mr Krupp said, "you've got no business bossing me around!"

"I'll have you know," said Tippy, "that I'm MORE than just a regular prisoner! I'm an art-*eest*! I was *handpicked* to build a robo – er, I mean, a *statue* by Warden Schmorden."

Suddenly, a rotund little man peeped his
bulbous, dandruff-speckled head out from
behind the green tarp. "Did somebody just say
my name?" he asked excitedly. It was Warden
Gordon B. Schmorden, the guardian and
chief jailer of Piqua State Penitentiary. Warden
Schmorden was known far and wide for his
cruelty and strictness. He once sentenced a
prisoner to a year of solitary confinement just
for ending a sentence with
a preposition.

Warden Schmorden was undoubtedly the most maniacally evil person anyone had ever met, but the injurious jailer had one fatal weakness: He was easily flattered. And that weakness was exactly what Tippy Tinkletrousers used to talk his way into making a giant statue of Warden Gordon Bordon Schmorden, to commemorate the ten-year anniversary of the Piqua State Penitentiary.

"Just leave everything to me," said Tippy at the start of the project, "and I'll construct the most stunningly handsome statue you've ever seen!"

"Really?" said the warden. "Can you make it extra tall and *extra* handsome?"

"Of course!" said Tippy.

"Wonderful, *WONDERFUL*!" cried Warden Schmorden. "How soon can you get started?"

"As soon as I get my supplies," said Tippy.

He handed the warden a carefully written
list of tools and materials.

"Hey!" said Warden Schmorden, looking
over the list. "Why do most of these supplies
come from the Mad Scientist Mini-Mall? What
do you need an *Emulsifying Sossilflange
Inhibitor* for? And what kind
of a statue uses a *Reverse-Somgobulating
Tracto-McFractionalizer*?"

"You know," said Tippy, "I don't tell you
how to run your prison – so don't tell me how
to build my statues!"

"Fair enough!" said Warden Schmorden.

CHAPTER 5
THE UNVEILING

One brisk evening in late October, the entire prison was yawning with excitement. The prisoners had all gathered in the bleachers under a clear, moonlit sky, as the prison band played a slow, reverent and deeply moving rendition of "Whoomp! (There It Is)". After everyone dried their eyes, Warden Gordon Bordon Schmorden stepped on to the stage to congratulate himself. He proudly bragged about his great humility, confessed his intense hatred of intolerant people and spoke for hours about his legendary brevity.

Then the moment of truth arrived. Tippy
Tinkletrousers's statue was finally ready to be
shown to the world.

With great theatrical flair, Tippy proudly
strutted out to the courtyard and grabbed hold
of the giant green tarp.

"Gentlemen and gentlemen," he
announced. "It gives me great pleasure to get
the heck out of here!"

Tippy pulled on the tarp and revealed his
creation.

"Hey!" shouted Warden Gordon Bordon
Schmorden. "That statue doesn't have a head!"

"It's not a statue!" yelled Tippy, as he
climbed a tall ladder up to the cockpit on top.
"It's a giant Robo-Suit! And after I escape
from this horrible prison, I'm going to put
an end to that nonsensical nuisance, Captain
Underpants!"

Tippy wiggled into the tiny cockpit and started up the engines. Suddenly, the colossal contraption came to life. Its mighty chest heaved as its gigantic, gorilla-like arms swayed threateningly.

"SOUND THE ALARMS!" screamed Warden Schmorden. "STOP THAT GUY!"

Armed guards ran in every direction while sirens wailed and prisoners screamed for their lives. Massive searchlights swept across the sky as the metallic behemoth took its first thunderous steps towards freedom.

Suddenly, Tippy stopped and thought for a moment. "Hey! I know where I saw that guy before!" he said. Tippy searched the crowds of panicking prisoners until he found the one he was looking for.

The giant hand of Tippy's Robo-Suit reached down and plucked Mr Krupp from the crowd.

"I *KNEW* I'd recognized you from somewhere!" said Tippy. "You're the principal of that school I shrank last year!"

"Oh, yeeeaaaah!" said Mr Krupp. "I remember you now! You're that *Professor Poopypants* guy."

"MY NAME IS *NOT* PROFESSOR POOPYPANTS!" screamed the angry villain. "*That* was a ridiculous name! So I changed it to Tippy Tinkletrousers!"

"Gee, that's a *lot* better!" said Mr Krupp sarcastically.

Tippy glared into Mr Krupp's defiant eyes. "I shall ignore your *impudence* on one condition!" Tippy said. "Tell me where I can find George Beard and Harold Hutchins!"

"George and Harold?" asked Mr Krupp, as he dangled precariously from Tippy's giant robotic fingertips. "What do you want with those two?"

"Those boys have *something* to do with Captain Underpants!" said Tippy. "I've seen them all together. They know each other, *I'm sure of it*!"

"Well, they should be pretty easy to find!" said Mr Krupp. "They're both locked up at the Piqua Juvenile Detention Centre!"

"They're in *juvie*, eh?" said Tippy, with a sinister smirk. "Then that's where *we're* gonna go!"

Tippy clutched Mr Krupp tightly in his robotic fist as he stomped forward, crushing the armoured watchtower and smashing through Cell Block B.

"Freeze, or we'll shoot!" shouted the guards.

"How about if *I* shoot and *YOU* freeze?" said Tippy, as he pressed a button on his control panel, causing a giant door in the chest of his Robo-Suit to swing open. A massive laser shooter poked out from the mechanical depths of the Robo-Suit and zapped the armed guards. Suddenly, they were transformed into frozen statues.

"*WHAT DID YOU JUST DO?*" screamed Mr
Krupp hysterically.

"Oh, relax," said Tippy. "It's just my Freezy-
Beam 4000. It temporarily freezes whatever it
zaps, for as long as I choose. Those guards will
thaw out in about ten minutes and they'll be
perfectly fine."

Tippy's heaving, mechanical monstrosity
thundered through the prison parking lot,
battering buses and crushing cars as it headed
towards the Piqua Juvenile Detention Centre.

"I just don't get it," said Mr Krupp. "What's so important about Captain Underpants?"

"That ridiculous superhero foiled my plot to take over the planet and enslave humanity!" shouted Tippy. "He's the reason I got locked up!"

"Everybody knows that," said Mr Krupp, "but what's going to stop him from defeating you again?"

"Oh, don't you worry your sweaty little head about that," said Tippy. "I've got a few tricks up my sleeve *this time*!"

CHAPTER 6

CALLING CAPTAIN UNDERPANTS

Meanwhile, across town at the Piqua Juvenile
Detention Centre, George and Harold were
getting ready for bed.

"You know," said George, "I don't really
mind being stuck here in juvie."

"Yeah," said Harold. "It's not much
different from our old school . . . except that
they have library books here."

"And a music teacher," said George.

"And an art teacher," said Harold.

As the two boys discussed the similarities between elementary school and forced confinement in a harsh, authoritarian penal institute, they heard the sounds of booming footsteps getting louder and louder.

Soon, their entire building began to shake violently with each thundering stride.

George and Harold dashed to their windows and saw Tippy's terrifying Robo-Suit stomping towards them, freezing anyone and everything that stood in its way.

"Oh, NO!" screamed Harold. "We're DOOMED!"

Tippy stopped at the main entrance to the centre and demanded to speak with whoever was in charge. After a few minutes, the centre's administrator, Director Hector Schmector, showed up nervously at the door.

"Umm. . ." said Director Schmector. "M-M-May I help you?"

"Do you have two kids in there named George Beard and Harold Hutchins?" shouted Tippy.

"Uh, yeah," said Director Schmector.
"Those two kids are nothing but trouble.
They're always pulling pranks, too! I mean,
you can't sit on a toilet around here without
getting ketchup sprayed in your underwear!
And last week, they—"

"JUST HAND THEM OVER!" Tippy
interrupted.

"Hey, no *prob*!" Director Schmector
chuckled, trying to sound cool.

401

Director Hector Schmector pranced
excitedly to George and Harold's cell, grabbed
them by the arms and escorted them to the
front door. "This'll teach you for putting
hair remover in my shampoo!" said Director
Schmector.

Hector tossed the boys outside and locked
the door. George and Harold stood trembling
before Tippy's massive Robo-Suit as the
crazed inventor chuckled menacingly.

"Hello, George and Harold!" crowed Tippy.
"Remember me?"

The boys were too frightened to speak.

"Hey, Tippy," said Mr Krupp. "You don't need me any more, do you? I mean, I told you where you could find the brats, right? You can let me go now, right?"

"I guess so," said Tippy. He set Mr Krupp down on the ground by George and Harold.

"Ha!" Mr Krupp laughed. "I never thought I'd be happy to see *you two kids* again! You bubs are in BIG TROUBLE NOW!"

Almost without thinking, George and Harold reached out their hands and snapped their fingers.

SNAP!
SNAP!

Suddenly, a ridiculously optimistic smile spread across Mr Krupp's face.

"Hey!" cried Tippy. "What's going on down there?"

What George and Harold knew, and what Tippy was about to discover, was that Mr Krupp was transforming into the world's greatest superhero: Captain Underpants.

Quickly, he wiggled out of his purple prison jumpsuit, flipped his shoes away, and peeled off his sweaty toupee. The only thing missing was his cape. He looked around the detention centre but couldn't find anything suitable. "I can't be a superhero without a cape," said Captain Underpants.

"You're OK!" George assured him.

"Yeah!" said Harold. "You don't need a cape! Seriously!"

"Sorry," said the Captain, "but ya *gotta* look fine if you're gonna fight crime!"

And with no time to spare, Captain Underpants flew off to find a cape.

"That – *that guy was Captain Underpants*?!!?" cried Tippy.

"Doyee!" said George.

"AAAUGH!" screamed Tippy. "I JUST HAD HIM IN MY HAND!!! I COULD HAVE CRUSHED HIM!!!"

Again, George responded with the only intelligent word that could possibly be applied in such a situation: *"Doyee!"*

Meanwhile, Captain Underpants had flown
to a nearby shopping centre, which was
having its Semiannual Lazy Storytelling Sale.

"Quick!" cried Captain Underpants. "Do you
guys sell superhero capes?"

"You betcha!" said the employee cheerfully.
"They're in aisle thirty-nine between the diaries
and the wizard hats!"

"Awesome!" cried Captain Underpants.

In no time at all, our hero found a cape, tied
it around his neck, and flew off into the night
to face his mortal enemy.

CHAPTER 7

TIPPY'S TROUSER TROUBLES

Meanwhile, back at the Piqua Juvenile
Detention Centre, Tippy Tinkletrousers was in
a tizzy! He grabbed George and Harold in his
mighty, robotic hands and demanded some
answers.

"Tell me everything you know about
Captain Underpants," screamed Tippy, "or I'll
squish you kids like a couple of blueberries!"

"Well," said George, "he's really strong!"

"And," said Harold, "he's really powerful!"

"Yes, yes," said Tippy. "What *else* is he?"

"*He's right behind you!*" said George and Harold simultaneously.

Tippy turned quickly, but not quickly enough. Captain Underpants swung his flabby fist and bashed Tippy right in the jaw.

The force of the blow sent Tippy's Robo-Suit flying over the top of the Juvenile Detention Centre and into one of Piqua's many downtown skyscrapers.

George and Harold flew from the grip of Tippy's Robo-Fists and landed safely in some nearby bushes.

"I'll keeeeel YOU!" screamed Tippy, as
he pulled himself up and lunged at Captain
Underpants. The chest panel of the Robo-Suit
flipped open and a brilliant burst of energy
from the Freezy-Beam 4000 shot out at the
Waistband Warrior. But Captain Underpants
was too quick. He zipped and zinged, expertly
avoiding every frozen energy beam that burst
from the belly of the beastly Robo-Suit.

"Oh, *Tippy*!" called Captain Underpants, as he sat coyly atop a nearby skyscraper. "I'm up here!"

Tippy turned quickly and zapped his Freezy-Beam 4000 at the skyscraper, covering it with a thick casing of ice. But Captain Underpants had been too fast. He had zinged away just in time.

Captain Underpants flew several blocks away, to the swing set at the playground of Jerome Horwitz Elementary School. Robo-Tippy ran after him.

"Yoo-hoo! *Tippy-Tip!*" Captain Underpants sang, as he swung playfully from a swing. "Will you give me a push?"

Tippy leaped over the school and landed in the football field.

He zapped his Freezy-Beam 4000 again, this time covering the swing set with a thick coating of ice. But again, Captain Underpants had zanged away just in time.

ZANG!

"Heeeere, Tippy, Tippy, Tippy!" called
Captain Underpants again, as he lounged
lazily between Tippy's giant robotic feet.
"I'm down here now! Could I have some ice,
please?"

"Why you little —" screamed Tippy, as he
bent over and zapped his Freezy-Beam 4000
down between his feet.

Of course, Captain Underpants was long gone before the ice beam reached the ground. Unfortunately for Tippy, however, his Robo-Feet weren't.

Tippy's giant Robo-Feet and Robo-Legs were now encased in a huge, shimmering iceberg. He pulled with all his might, but his whole lower half was frozen to the football field. Tippy was stuck.

ZONG!

CHAPTER 8

BREAK IN TWO: ELECTRIC BOOGALOO

"NOOOOOO!" screamed Tippy. He ducked his head beneath the cockpit of the Robo-Suit and disappeared down a stairwell into the intricate innards of his intimidating invention.

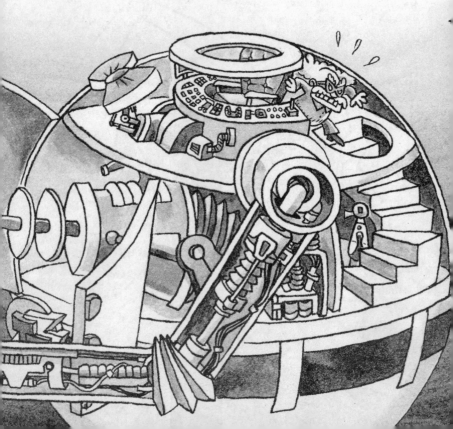

Captain Underpants grabbed the arms of
the Robo-Suit and began to pull. Harder and
harder he tugged until, one by one, the rivets
in the Robo-Suit's thick steel belt began to pop.
The harder Captain Underpants yanked, the
more the Robo-Suit began to break in two.

The shrieking sounds of twisting metal
reverberated around Tippy as he traversed the
crumbling staircase. His only chance was to
make it down to the lower half of the Robo-
Suit before Captain Underpants pulled it apart.

With no time to spare, Tippy dashed into
the Robo-Trousers, just as the Robo-Suit
broke in two.

"You haven't seen the last of me!" Tippy yelled, as he closed the emergency hatch on the Robo-Trousers. Then, Tippy set his Tinkle-Time Travelometer to "Five Years Ago" and pressed the "Away We Go!" button.

Suddenly, sparks of blue lightning began emanating from the Robo-Trousers. The massive bolts crackled loudly and grew more and more intense until finally, Tippy and his Robo-Trousers were enveloped in a giant ball of blue lightning.

A blinding flash turned the night sky into day for a sliver of a second and then it was all over. Tippy and his Robo-Trousers had disappeared, leaving only an empty mound of ice behind. The crazed inventor and his terrifying trousers would never be seen again after that night. They would, however, be seen exactly five years *before* that night. . .

But before I can tell you that story, we have to go back *even further*. . .

CHAPTER 9

EXACTLY FIVE YEARS, ELEVEN DAYS, FOURTEEN HOURS, AND SIX MINUTES AGO...

This is Harold Hutchins.

Harold is six years old and he lives with his mom and sister at 1520 Vine Street in Piqua, Ohio.

Harold's parents had just gotten divorced and his dad had moved to Nevada about six months ago. None of this had been easy for Harold. He didn't talk about it. In fact, Harold Hutchins didn't talk much at all. He kept to himself, mostly, and drew pictures. Lots and lots of pictures.

Harold liked to draw monsters and superheroes. The monsters he created were evil and ferocious, and his superheroes were always virtuous and brave. They were never far away when you needed them.

Harold loved getting lost in his wonderful paper-and-pencil adventures, where the good guys always won and the bad guys always ended up getting the "kick in the butt" that they deserved.

Today had started out just like any ordinary school day. Harold got dressed and ate his breakfast, trying hard not to think about the tough day that lay ahead of him. Harold was in kindergarten at Jerome Horwitz Elementary School, and he hated every minute of it. His teacher was mean, the bullies were jerks, and the principal was just plain *evil*. The best Harold could do was try to "fit in" and not draw any unnecessary attention to himself. He brushed his teeth and carefully placed his pencils and his favourite drawings into his backpack, unaware that today was going to be a day that would change his life for ever.

Harold's mom helped him put his backpack on at the front door.

"Maybe you'll make a friend at school today," she said cheerfully.

"Nah," said Harold, emotionless. "I don't think so."

"What about that little boy next door who moved in last weekend?" said Harold's mom. "What's his name?"

Harold shrugged. He had seen the boy once or twice, but they hadn't actually met.

"Maybe you should go over and introduce yourself," said Harold's mom. "Wouldn't it be nice to have a friend who lives next door?"

Harold shrugged again.

Harold's mom hugged him and kissed the top of his head. She got two dollars out of her purse and handed them to Harold. "This is for your lunch, OK, honey?" she said. "I don't want you using this money at the candy machine or the pop machine!"

"I won't," said Harold.

That much was true. Harold knew his lunch money would never make it to the candy machine or the pop machine. Harold's two dollars usually never even made it into the school. They were always taken away from him by a sixth-grade bully named Kipper.

Kipper Krupp was the biggest and meanest kid at Jerome Horwitz Elementary School. He was the captain of the wrestling team *AND* the nephew of the school principal, so everybody treated him like *royalty*.

Kipper's three creepy friends, Loogie, Bugg, and Finkstein, also got special treatment, and they all paraded up and down the school hallways like they owned the place.

Every day, Kipper and his three friends stole lunch money from the kindergartners. Most of the kids just handed it over without question. It was a lot less trouble (and much less painful) than getting a wedgie or a punch in the stomach. Kipper Krupp loved to terrorize kindergartners and there was nothing anybody could do about it. If Kipper ever got into a jam, all he had to do was call on his uncle, Principal Krupp.

"Uncle Benny!" Kipper would cry. "That kindergartner just hit my fist with her stomach!"

"Oh, she *DID*, did she?" Mr Krupp would yell, turning to the small child writhing in pain on the floor. "How DARE you hurt my nephew's fist?!!?" Mr Krupp had a ZERO-TOLERANCE policy in place at Jerome Horwitz Elementary School and he was very strict about it. He had once suspended a third grader just for saying the word "gun". To be honest, the boy had actually said the word "gum", but it *sounded* a lot like "gun", and there was no room for common sense when it came to ZERO TOLERANCE.

Harold knew from experience that the wisest thing to do was to stay out of Kipper's way, so his daily walk to school became more like an obstacle course. He quickly ran in spurts, dashing from trash can to mailbox to tree, hiding behind anything he could find, just in case Kipper and his friends were nearby.

The worst section of Harold's mad dash to school was the intersection of Dogwood Drive and Rosita Lane. There was nowhere to hide between the big tree by the coffee shop and the sign at the gas station across the street. He just had to wait for the walk signal, run for it and hope for the best. Most days, Harold was lucky. But his luck was about to run out.

Harold crouched quietly behind the coffee shop tree, watching the traffic lights, concentrating on the cars and looking out for Kipper. It was very stressful. After a couple of minutes, the cars came to a stop, the walk signal lit up and Harold took one last glance left and right. It was now or never. He jumped up and ran across the street as fast as he could go. When he reached the other side of the street, Harold leaped behind the display sign in front of the gas station. He had made it! He was safe . . . *or so he thought.*

"HEY, YOU STUPID KID!" shouted Billy Bill, the owner of the gas station. "GIT AWAY FROM THAT SIGN!" Harold's heart was pounding in his throat as Billy Bill stomped towards him and grabbed the back of his T-shirt. He yanked Harold out from behind the sign, making a terrible scene. "THAT SIGN IS A VALUABLE PIECE OF MERCHANDISE," Billy Bill screamed, "NOT A *TOY* FOR YOU TO PLAY WITH!"

"I'm sorry, I'm sorry!" Harold whispered, frantically trying to pull away. But it was too late. Billy Bill's loud shouting had caught the attention of Kipper Krupp and his three creepy thugs. The four bullies strutted across the street towards Harold.

"Hey, kid!" yelled Kipper. "Why are you bothering this nice man?"

"I'm sorry!" Harold said again, looking down. Billy Bill released Harold with a shove, causing him to fall to the ground.

"You boys better take care of your little friend there," Billy Bill said, "or I'm gonna call the cops on him!"

"Don't worry, Mister," said Kipper with an evil grin. "We'll take *good* care of him!"

Kipper yanked Harold up by his arm while Loogie pulled Harold's backpack open and started rummaging through it. "Hey, look! I found his lunch money," said Loogie.

"Gimme it!" yelled Kipper. Loogie dutifully put the money into Kipper's moist, dirty hand.

None of this behaviour appeared to disturb Billy Bill at all. In fact, he seemed to enjoy watching it.

"You gotta learn to stick up for yourself, boy," Billy Bill said to Harold, chuckling, "or people are gonna bully you your whole life!"

The four thugs dragged Harold across the street, towards the school parking lot. Harold's luck was running out. But fortunately, as we all know, luck has a way of changing. And Harold's bad luck was about to change in a very BIG way.

CHAPTER 10
MEET GEORGE

This is George Beard.

George is five-and-three-quarters years old. He and his parents had just moved from Michigan into the house next door to Harold and his family. George was what adults like to call a "precocious" child. His mother had taught him to read and write when he was four years old, and he currently scored higher on tests than most children twice his age.

George's former teachers had suggested that he skip ahead to the third grade, but his parents decided it would be better if George stayed in a classroom with kids his own age. To this day, George's parents were still not sure if they had made the right decision. On the one hand, George had developed good social skills and had been well liked by his classmates. That was good. On the other hand, George was bored in class and often got into mischief. That was bad.

George had never really liked school very much. He preferred riding his skateboard, watching monster movies and reading comics and graphic novels. George liked writing stories, too. He had filled up more than twenty spiral notebooks with marvellously silly adventure stories that he had written all by himself.

Many of George's stories had gotten him into trouble when he read them out loud at his old school. His classmates loved them, but his teachers thought they were rude, violent and totally inappropriate.

"I hope things will be better here in Ohio," said George's mother, as she helped him get ready for his very first day of classes at Jerome Horwitz Elementary School. "Your father and I bought you this nice tie to wear at school today."

"A *TIE*?" cried George. "Kids don't wear ties!"

"Well, *you're* going to wear one," said George's mother. "I want you to make a good *first impression*!"

"Aw, come on, Mom!" said George. "Ties are for nerds!"

"Oh, for heaven's sake!" said George's mom. "Your father wears a tie. Is he a nerd?"

"Umm . . . *kind of*," said George.

"Don't be ridiculous!" said George's mom. "You're wearing a tie and that's *FINAL*!"

"Rats!" said George.

George put his backpack on and reluctantly hugged his mom at the door. (He was still a little upset about the whole "tie" thing.)

"Have a good first day at school, dear," said George's mom.

"Mm-hmmm," said George.

George grabbed his skateboard from the bushes by the driveway and started off towards school. It was about five blocks away and the sidewalks were mostly smooth with hardly any pebbles. Good for skateboarding.

The ride to school had been very pleasant, actually, until George reached the corner of Dogwood Drive and Rosita Lane. There was some kind of commotion going on in front of the gas station across the street and George watched it intently as he waited for the traffic light to change. He saw the gas station guy shove a yellow-haired kid to the ground. Then he saw some mean-looking kids yank the boy up and steal his money. This was not good.

Finally, the light changed and George walked across the street towards the gas station. He stood by the display sign while the attendant laughed at the yellow-haired kid and told him he needed to learn to stick up for himself. George was furious.

CHAPTER 11

FURIOUS GEORGE

There is not a whole lot you can do when you are a little kid who encounters injustice. Your natural desire is to set things right, but that can often backfire, resulting in even *greater* injustices. The sad truth is, big people usually have all of the power. You can't force anybody to be kind or fair or honourable, especially if you're only forty-three inches tall and weigh only fifty pounds.

That's why it's important to be smart.

George Beard had just witnessed the most hostile and unfair thing he had ever seen. The bad guys outnumbered him by five to one and outweighed him by probably 700 pounds. But George was smarter than all of them put together and he knew it.

As the bullies dragged Harold across the street, George looked around him for the best way to make things right. He focused in on the display sign next to him. The sign read FREE BRAKE INSPECTION. This was a busy intersection and George knew that a tiny change on this sign could create a great deal of pandemonium, so he reached over to the sign and removed the letters *k* and *e* from the word *brake*.

"HEY!" screamed Billy Bill. "YOU GIT
AWAY FROM THAT SIGN RIGHT NOW,
Y'HEAR?!!? WHAT IS *WRONG* WITH YOU
KIDS THESE DAYS?!!?"

Billy Bill marched over to George, yelling
and waving his hands in the air frantically. He
reached out to grab George by the shirt collar,
but he never got the chance.

At that very moment, a violet Volkswagen jumped the kerb and screeched up next to Billy Bill. Two old ladies flew out of the car, screaming at the top of their lungs!

"Free *BRA* inspection?!!?" shouted the driver, as she smacked Billy Bill over the head with her purse. "That's *OFFENSIVE*!!!"

"HOW *DARE* YOU?!!?" yelled the other lady, hitting Billy Bill with her cane. "Women are human beings, not *toys* for you to play with!"

"You're a MALE CHAUVINIST PIG!"
screamed a third lady, who had run over
from the coffee shop across the street with a
group of her angry female friends. They each
took turns kicking Billy Bill repeatedly in the
knees, as other women drivers slammed on
their brakes and rushed forward to join in the
ferocious female fight for equality.

"You gotta learn to stick up for yourself,"

George said to Billy Bill, smiling, "or people are gonna bully you your whole life!"

George walked past the giant traffic jam that was forming and ignored Billy Bill's tear-filled cries for mercy as the kicking and whacking and hair-pulling and foot-stomping continued. George was looking for that yellow-haired kid.

He skateboarded over to the elementary school and circled back towards the parking lot. There he saw Kipper and his creepy cohorts laughing and cheering as they tore up Harold's drawings and snapped each of his pencils in half.

"LEAVE HIM ALONE!" shouted George.

The sixth-grade bullies turned and looked at the tiny kindergartner who stood defiantly before them.

"Haw! Haw! Haw!" laughed Kipper. "Whatcha gonna do if we don't?"

"I'm gonna *Indiana Jones* ya!" George said, as he untied his tie and twirled it threateningly between his outstretched hands.

"GET HIM!" yelled Kipper. The bullies ran in for the attack and George let them have it.

CHAPTER 12

THE INCREDIBLY GRAPHIC VIOLENCE CHAPTER (IN FLIP-O-RAMA™)

Introducing
FLIP-O
This chapter contains scenes of intense brutality and is intended for mature audiences only!
For those of us who aren't very mature, we proudly introduce the art of FLIP-O-RAMA!

PiLKEY® BRAND
₵·RAMA

HERE'S HOW IT WORKS!

STEP 1

First, place your *left* hand inside the dotted lines marked "LEFT HAND HERE." Hold the book open *flat*.

STEP 2

Grasp the *right-hand* page with your right thumb and index finger (inside the dotted lines marked "RIGHT THUMB HERE").

STEP 3

Now *quickly* flip the right-hand page back and forth until the picture appears to be *animated*.

(For extra fun, try adding your own sound-effects!)

FLIP-O-RAMA

(pages 451 and 453)

Remember, flip *only* page 451.
While you are flipping, be sure you
can see the picture on page 451
and the one on page 453.
If you flip quickly, the two
pictures will start to look like
<u>one</u> *animated* picture.

Don't forget to
add your own sound-effects!

LEFT HAND HERE

THE KIPPER
WHIPPER

451

RIGHT
THUMB
HERE

RIGHT
INDEX
FINGER
HERE

THE KIPPER
WHIPPER

Kipper screamed like a giant,
blubbering baby and ran for his life.
Bugg and Loogie were up next.

LEFT HAND HERE

THE ATTACKER
SMACKER

RIGHT
THUMB
HERE

RIGHT
INDEX
FINGER
HERE

THE ATTACKER
SMACKER

"Let's get out of here!" screamed Loogie
and Bugg through their tears.
Finkstein opened up a trash bin and
the four bullies tried to scramble inside.
But they weren't fast enough!

LEFT HAND HERE

THE TORMENTER
PREVENTER

459

RIGHT THUMB HERE

THE TORMENTER
PREVENTER

CHAPTER 13

THE DETENTION

"I don't want you guys messing with me ever again!" George said firmly, as the bullies squealed in high-pitched terror. "And that yellow-haired kid is off-limits, too! You mess with us, you answer to *The TIE*!"

George snapped his tie in the air one last time, causing the four sobbing sixth graders to shriek like baboons.

"*Uh-Uh-Uncle BENNY!*" Kipper wailed through his tears.

Suddenly, Mr Krupp came storming out
of the building. *"WHAT'S GOING ON OUT
HERE?"* he screamed.

"That little kid beat us up!" Kipper sobbed.

"Oh, he *DID*, did he?" yelled Mr Krupp, as
he grabbed George by his arm. "I don't take
kindly to *bullies* in this school!"

"They're the bullies!" cried Harold,
pointing at Kipper and his three frightened
friends. "Those guys were just about to beat
that kid up. . . He was just defending himself!"

Mr Krupp reached over and grabbed Harold
by his arm. "I don't like *LIARS,* either!" he
growled.

463

Mr Krupp yanked both boys to the detention room. "You two troublemakers are going to stay here until you've learned your lesson!" he shouted, then slammed the door.

"So much for a good first impression," said George.

The two boys sat in silence for several minutes. Harold opened his backpack and took out a notebook and the pointy half of one of his broken pencils. He started to draw.

"What grade are you in?" asked George.

"Kindergarten," said Harold.

"Me, too," said George. "I'm new. We just moved here three days ago."

"Oh," said Harold. "I think you live next door to my house."

"Really?" said George.

George glanced over and noticed that Harold was drawing a giant monster.

"Hey, you're a good drawer," George said.

"Thanks," said Harold.

George watched as Harold drew a flying hero zapping the monster with a laser beam.

"Cool!" said George, pointing to the superhero. "What's that guy's name?"

Harold shrugged. "He doesn't have a name."

"How come?" asked George.

Harold shrugged again. "It's just a picture," he said. "It's not really a story."

"Oh," said George.

George watched intently as Harold finished his picture. When he was done, Harold folded the page back and started drawing a new picture on the next page.

"Um . . . do you want to draw, too?" Harold asked. "I have some more pencils. They're broken, but the pointy parts still work OK."

"No," said George. "I can't draw good. I'm a writer."

"Oh," said Harold. He tore some fresh pages out from the back of his notebook and handed them to George. "Here. You can write on these if you want."

George took the papers and thought for a long time. Then he wrote *The Adventures of Dog Man* at the top of the first page. At the bottom he wrote *By George and. . .*

"Hey, what's your name, kid?" George asked.

"Harold," said Harold.

George wrote Harold's name down at the bottom. "I'm gonna write a comic book," said George. "You can draw the pictures, OK?"

"Umm . . . OK," said Harold.

And that is how George and Harold became friends and started their publishing empire on the very same day.

Soon the Dockter came in with sad news.
BOO HOO
Im am sorey Greg But your Body is Dying.
your Head is Dying Too, Cop.
rats I shure hate my Dying head.
But then
Hay I got a idea
nurse Lady

BUT NOBUDY new that somebudy was waching
Somebudy evil!
It was Petey the worlds most evilest cat.
HAW HAW HAW NOW I KNOW DOG MANS WEAKNISS
So Petey invented a evil vac-kume Robot.

GOOD BOY DOG man!!! Shake!!!
Polis cheef
whine whine whine
GOOD IDea! Lets have some wine!!!
PC
non-alckaholick wine
Horay for DOG man!!!
The End

CHAPTER 15
THE PLAN

Mr Krupp's day had been very busy, and he'd completely forgotten all about the two boys he had banished to the detention room. By the time the final bell rang at 2:45, George and Harold had finished their very first comic book.

"Hey, this comic book turned out pretty good," said George.

"Yep," said Harold, smiling.

"I bet we could make copies of this and sell them for twenty-five cents each!" said George.

The two boys gathered their things and walked out the front door of the school.

"We should start our own comic book company," said Harold.

"Let's do it!" said George. "We can call it Tree House Comix, Inc.!"

"Why *Tree House*?" asked Harold.

"Cuz my dad is building me a tree house in our backyard!" said George. "It's going to have electricity and a TV and everything! We can make our comic books up there!"

"Awesome!" said Harold.

George and Harold walked by the trash bin where Kipper and his friends were just about to administer *killer wedgies* to a couple of kindergartners.

"Oh, *Kippy*," called George.

The bullies turned and saw George reaching for his tie. Suddenly, their eyes filled with horror. They released their prey and ran away, waving their arms and yipping like wiener dogs.

"I think I'm going to wear a tie every day from now on!" said George.

"I think that's a good idea," said Harold.

As George and Harold walked home, the
two friends talked about their favourite movies
and games, which videos were the funniest,
and what kind of bubble gum blew the best
bubbles.

"Mmmm," said Harold. "All that talk about
bubble gum is making me hungry!"

"C'mon over to my house," said George.
"I make a *mean* peanut-butter-and-gummy-
worm sandwich!"

"Really?" said Harold.

"Yep!" George said. "The secret is the
chocolate syrup!"

"OK," said Harold.

Soon the boys reached George's house
and headed for the backyard. George's dad
was hard at work building George's new tree
house.

"Hi, Pop!" said George.

"Hey, buddy," said George's dad, "how was your first day at your new school?"

"OK," said George.

"And who's your new friend?" George's dad asked.

"This is Harold," said George. "He's a good drawer."

"Hello, Harold," said George's dad.

"Hi," said Harold.

"Well, we've got a lot of work to do, Pop," said George. "Do you want us to bring you a peanut-butter-and-gummy-worm sandwich?"

"Er – no, thank you," said George's dad.

The two new friends walked into George's house, made some sandwiches and got right to work. George and Harold knew it was up to them to put a stop to Kipper Krupp's reign of terror. So they made a long list of Kipper's strengths and weaknesses to get a better understanding of their mortal enemy.

After a few minutes, Harold began to feel discouraged.

"This is terrible," said Harold. "Kipper Krupp has so many *strengths*! I can only think of one weakness!"

"What's that?" asked George.

"Well, he's kinda dumb," said Harold.

George smiled and wrote down *kinda dumb* under *weaknesses*. "That's all we need," said George.

CHAPTER 16
SUPER SPIES

The next day at school, Harold stuck close to George. The two boys spent their every free moment spying on Kipper and gathering as much information as they could about their enemy.

They wrote down Kipper's locker number and the type of padlock he used. They took note of Kipper's schedule and paid special attention to what he normally did between classes. They took measurements and even stayed after school to spy on Kipper's wrestling practices. By the end of the week, George and Harold knew Kipper's schedule better than Kipper knew it.

Kipper Krupp was a creature of habit. Every day, he did the exact same things at the exact same times. At the end of every school day, Kipper would go to his locker and unlock his heavy-duty padlock with a key he kept on a thick, metal chain around his neck. Kipper would place his padlock on top of his locker, then open the locker door. Next, Kipper would empty his pockets, putting his valuables inside the locker. His mobile phone always went on the top shelf, and the money he'd stolen from the kindergartners would always get crammed into a duffel bag at the bottom of the locker. Finally, Kipper would grab his padlock from the top of the locker, put it back on the door, and click it shut to lock it.

After wrestling practice, Kipper would go back to his locker and unlock it the very same way. He'd retrieve his mobile phone, grab his heavy-duty padlock from the top of his locker, and put it back on the door. Finally, he'd click it shut to lock everything back up again. Surprisingly, Kipper usually left all of his stolen money in his locker every night. Perhaps Kipper thought the money was safest in his locker. Nobody could open that locker without a key; nobody but Kipper had the key, and Kipper *never* took the key off of his neck . . . not even in the *shower*!

"We'll never get that key away from Kipper," said Harold, as the two boys walked up the aisles of the local hardware store.

"We don't need the key," said George. "We just need this!" George picked up a brand-new padlock from the home security section. "This is the exact same kind of padlock that Kipper uses on his locker," said George.

"But it won't have the same key," said Harold. "Each one has a different key!"

"I know," said George.

"So how is *that* padlock going to help us?" asked Harold.

"You'll see. . ." said George, smiling.

494

After the boys paid for their brand-new heavy-duty padlock, they went to the toy shop across the street.

Down at the end of aisle three, near the beads and jewellery, George found what he was looking for: a Susie Sunshine Friendship Bracelet Kit.

"What is *THAT* for?" asked Harold.

"We've gotta make a couple of friendship bracelets this weekend," said George.

"Why? What for?" said Harold.

"You'll see. . ." said George, smiling even more.

That weekend, George and Harold spent a lot of time drawing up plans and designing pranks that would help put an end to the bully situation at Jerome Horwitz Elementary School. Then the two boys went through their homes, collecting everything they needed for the job. George found a long roll of shelf-lining paper in his kitchen and measured it carefully.

"Hey, Mom, can we have this?" said George. "It's for school."

"I suppose so," said George's mom.

Harold found some old trousers and dress shoes that his dad had left behind when he moved away. He was pretty sure his dad wouldn't mind if they nailed them to George's wooden stilts.

"I still don't understand how we're going to hide these stilts in the school," said George, as he practiced walking on them.

"You'll see . . ." said Harold, who knew a few tricks of his own.

CHAPTER 17

MONDAY

On Monday morning, the boys woke up early, gathered their supplies and headed to school about fifteen minutes before the rest of the students started to arrive. George and Harold carried their stilts and supplies into the boys' bathroom upstairs and placed them inside one of the empty stalls.

Finally, they closed the stall door and locked it.

If you were standing outside the stall, looking underneath the door, it appeared as if somebody was sitting down in there *taking care of business*. George and Harold knew that nobody would dare go near this stall, so it was now the safest place in the school to hide stuff.

Soon the students began arriving and the day started pretty much like normal. Mr Krupp marched up and down the hallways screaming and making children cry, Kipper and his creeps stole money and distributed wedgies to the kindergartners, and a general feeling of hopelessness and despair filled the morning air.

At lunchtime, as usual, the downtrodden kindergartners sat at their table with no food at all. Mr Krupp stomped up to the kindergarten table and started getting angry. "How come you kids never have any food at lunchtime?" he shouted.

"Um. . ." said one kid, "we're on diets."

"Oh," said Mr Krupp, as he pulled his belt up over his giant stomach. "Well, good!" he said. "It's important to stay fit and healthy like me!"

In the afternoon, George and Harold asked
to be excused so they could use the bathroom.
They only had about five minutes to set things
up, so they had to hurry. Harold opened the
locked door of their secret bathroom stall, and
George climbed up on the stilts. Quickly, they
sneaked out into the hallway.

George stilt-walked over to Kipper's locker,
and Harold handed him the long spool of shelf-
lining paper. Carefully, George placed the paper
on top of the lockers and rolled it down to the
end. The paper flipped over the edge of the
locker tops and rolled down the side. Harold
caught it and taped it to the side of the lockers,
marking off some measurements
with a ruler.

George put the padlock that he and Harold had bought on the end of the paper, two lockers down from Kipper's. They were ready. Quickly, they put their supplies back into the bathroom stall, locked the door and hurried back to their classroom.

At the end of the day, Kipper walked to his locker as usual. He unlocked his lock with the key hanging around his neck, then put his padlock on top of his locker (right on top of the long roll of paper). George and Harold were standing about six lockers away, where Harold had taped the end of the paper to the side of the long row of lockers. Now came the tricky part.

As Harold provided "cover", George
carefully pulled at the long roll of paper.
The paper began to move. Kipper's padlock,
which was just above Kipper's head, began to
move away from Kipper. George and Harold's
padlock, which was two lockers away, began
moving *towards* Kipper. Harold had measured
everything carefully, so George knew to pull
the paper exactly twenty-four inches.

When he was finished pulling, the new padlock was directly above Kipper's locker.

Kipper had just finished stuffing all of his stolen money into his duffel bag. He put his mobile phone on the top shelf of his locker, closed the door, then reached up and grabbed George and Harold's padlock. Next he closed the door and clicked the new padlock on securely.

"Let's boogie!" said Kipper to his buddies, and they strutted to the gymnasium to get ready for wrestling practice.

"That was *AWESOME*!" said Harold.

"Yeah," said George. "But we've still got a lot of work to do!"

George and Harold waited patiently until almost everybody had gone home. Some kids were still in the gym, or outside, or in the chess club downstairs, but the hallways and bathrooms were empty.

George and Harold sneaked over to Kipper's locker, unlocked their padlock and opened the door.

Harold unzipped Kipper's duffel bag and emptied all of the stolen money on to the floor.

"Whoa!" said Harold. "There must be a thousand dollars here!" Harold quickly scooped up the stolen cash while George typed on Kipper's mobile phone.

"What are you doing with that phone?" asked Harold.

"I'm sending a text to Kipper's three goons!" said George.

Once the money was safe and the texts were sent, George and Harold put everything back the way it was . . . *with two additions*. Harold put the Susie Sunshine Friendship Bracelet Kit in Kipper's locker, and George placed an envelope beside Kipper's phone.

Finally, George grabbed Kipper's padlock from the top of the lockers, closed the door, and locked it with Kipper's own padlock. Then they set everything up so it would be ready for tomorrow afternoon.

"Let's get out of here," Harold said nervously.

"Just one more thing," said George.

Quickly, the boys sneaked into the gym locker room and left a second envelope inside one of Kipper's smelly shoes. Then they hurried out of the school and headed for home.

"I kinda wish we could stay and watch the fireworks," said Harold.

"I think it's better if we're not there," said George. "Things are about to get ugly!"

CHAPTER 18

THINGS GET UGLY

Kipper found the envelope in his shoe just after wrestling practice ended. He opened it. Inside were two friendship bracelets and a note addressed to him. Kipper proudly slipped each friendship bracelet on to his wrist and admired it. He couldn't wait to show his buddies. . .

. . .who were all out in the hallway staring at their mobile phones in shock.

"Look what I got!" Kipper said, proudly waving his wrist at his goons.

Kipper's friends, who were all reading the same text message on their phones, looked up at Kipper with their mouths hanging open in disbelief.

"What?" said Kipper. "They're just friendship bracelets!"

Text message

From: Kipper Krupp

LeTs make Frendship braseLits! GeT ur Supplise @ my Locker! Whoevr makes the PrittyesT one gets a big kiss From ME !!!!!

Options   Back

Kipper's three friends looked at each other like Kipper had gone completely mad.

"I don't want to make friendship bracelets with you, dude," said Loogie.

"Me neither," said the other two thugs simultaneously.

"What are you talking about?" said Kipper. He unlocked his locker and opened it up.

"HEY! WHAT THE HECK IS THIS?!!?" Kipper screamed. "SOMEBODY'S BEEN IN MY LOCKER!!!"

Loogie, Bugg, and Finkstein saw the Susie Sunshine Friendship Bracelet Kit and shook their heads in disgust.

Kipper kicked the kit into the hallway and stomped on it. Then he tore open his duffel bag. It was empty.

"AAAAUGH!" Kipper screamed. "SOMEBODY *STOLE* ALL MY MONEY!"

Kipper looked up and down the hall frantically. "When I find out who's been in my locker, I'm gonna . . . I'm gonna. . ."

"*Kiss* them?" asked Finkstein. The other two thugs laughed.

Kipper grabbed Finkstein by his shirt collar and shook him back and forth like a rag doll. "WHAT ARE YOU TALKING ABOUT?!!?" he screamed.

"This!" said Finkstein. He showed Kipper the text that had been sent from Kipper's mobile phone.

"I-I-I DIDN'T WRITE THAT!!!" Kipper screamed.

"Well, what's up with those friendship bracelets on your wrist, then?" asked Bugg.

"The-the cheerleaders gave me those!" said Kipper.

At that very moment, a group of cheerleaders were coming in from practice outside.

"I'll prove it!" said Kipper. He showed the bracelets to the cheerleaders, waving his wrist at them like a lunatic. "You guys made these for me, right?" Kipper asked them, pointing desperately at the friendship bracelets.

The cheerleaders gave Kipper a strange look. "Eeeeww," said Wendy Swan, the head cheerleader.

Kipper blinked his eyes like a crazy person. He began breathing heavily. He clenched his fists and shook with rage. Kipper's friends glanced at each other, exchanging silent, worried looks. They each took a few steps backwards, as if they feared Kipper might explode.

"Hey, uh, we'll see you later, *Susie Sunshine*," said Loogie.

The three thugs walked away laughing, leaving Kipper alone and frenzied.

Finally, Kipper returned to his locker. He grabbed his mobile phone and found an envelope beside it.

Kipper tore the envelope open with insane rage and read the note inside.

CHAPTER 19

WHO IS WEDGIE MAGEE?

George and Harold stopped by the thrift store on their way home to buy a bunch of supplies for Tuesday. The checkout lady gave them a very strange look as they walked up to the till.

"What are all these dresses for?" asked the lady.

"They're for school," said Harold.

"Oh," said the lady.

When they got home, the two boys sat in George's bedroom and counted Kipper's stolen money. It totalled $916.00.

"I feel like Robin Hood!" said George. "What should we do with all this dough?"

"I think we should use it to buy lunches for all the kindergartners!" said Harold. "That's what it was supposed to be used for in the first place!"

George agreed. He picked up the phone and called the Piqua Pizza Palace. "Can you guys deliver pizzas to the elementary school around noon tomorrow?" he said. "Really? Awesome! We'll take five large cheese pizzas, five large pepperoni and five large black olive and pineapple." George discussed the details and arranged to drop off the payment in the morning. "We're all set for lunch tomorrow," said George.

"Cool!" said Harold.

The next morning on the way to school,
George and Harold walked by the Piqua Pizza
Palace. It wouldn't open until 11:00 A.M.,
but that didn't matter. George took out
an envelope filled with money, coupons,
instructions, and a tip for the delivery guy,
and dropped it through the mail slot on the
front door.

George and Harold had a very busy day
ahead of them. They got to school early and
unlocked the door to their secret bathroom
stall. As the two boys unloaded their supplies
and arranged their stilts, they heard the
sounds of the other students beginning to
arrive. Today *sounded* just like any other day,
but things at Jerome Horwitz Elementary
School were starting to change.

Kipper stood by the entrance of the school like normal, but he wasn't just stealing money from the kindergartners like he usually did. Today he also wanted information. He seemed a little anxious and shaky – like he hadn't gotten a lot of sleep the night before. Kipper's three buddies (who usually stuck close to his side) were keeping their distance from him. Loogie, Bugg and Finkstein all watched Kipper with worried looks on their faces.

Kipper grabbed every kid who came towards the door and asked them all the same question:

"Who is Wedgie Magee?"

Nobody outside the school had ever heard of Wedgie Magee. But inside the school, George and Harold were busy spreading rumours about this mysterious stranger.

"Did you hear about Wedgie Magee?" George asked Harold loudly near a group of gossipy girls.

"Yeah!" said Harold, even louder. "I heard Wedgie Magee is a *GHOST*!"

"Me, too!" said George. "I heard Wedgie Magee haunts the hallways of this very school, looking for REVENGE!"

"Revenge against who?" asked Harold intensely.

"Against Kipper Krupp!" cried George in a booming whisper.

The gossipy girls listened closely as George continued. "I heard that Kipper Krupp got *CURSED* by the ghost of Wedgie Magee!"

"Heavens, no!" cried Harold. "What for?"

"For being mean to kindergartners!" said George. "Wedgie Magee is the patron ghost of kindergartners!"

"I did not know that," said Harold. "Oh, poor Kipper! Poor, *poor* Kipper!"

George and Harold walked away, shaking their heads with pity. The wide-eyed group of gossipy girls had been rendered uncharacteristically speechless. Quickly, they began sending frantic texts to all of their friends about the horrible ghost of Wedgie Magee.

Within an hour, the whole school knew the terrible truth about Wedgie Magee and it didn't take long before the information made its way to Kipper and his friends.

"That's *stupid*!" said Kipper. "There's no such thing as ghosts!"

"Y-yeah," said Loogie, "but I heard he can go through walls and even lockers! Maybe the ghost stole all of that money yesterday!"

"That's a bunch of *BUNK*!" said Kipper. "What's a ghost gonna do with money?"

"M-m-maybe he'll give it back to the kindergartners!" said Finkstein. "I heard Wedgie Magee was a friend to all kindergartners!"

"Uh, excuse me," said a pizza delivery guy holding fifteen large pizza boxes. "I'm supposed to deliver these pizzas to the kindergartners. Do you guys know where the cafeteria is?"

"Down the hall," said Kipper. "Hey, who ordered those pizzas?"

"I don't know," said the delivery guy. "I never saw him. I think his name was *Wedgie* something."

Kipper gasped. "Y-you say you never saw him?"

"Nope!" said the delivery guy. "*Nobody's* ever seen him, but he's a pretty good tipper!"

CHAPTER 20

TUESDAY AFTERNOON

Lunchtime was a great success. All the kindergartners loved their pizza and pop, and nobody seemed to mind that it had all been bought and paid for by a ghost.

"Haunted pizza tastes the best!" said Freddie Moore and the other kindergartners couldn't have agreed more.

After school, Kipper unlocked his locker
and once again put his padlock on top of the
locker. And just like yesterday, George pulled
on the long strip of paper, switching Kipper's
padlock for their own.

Kipper grabbed George and Harold's
padlock, clicked it closed on his locker and
pulled hard to make sure it was really locked
tightly. It was.

Once the hallways were empty, George and Harold got back to work. George unlocked Kipper's locker while Harold filled it up with pretty, lacy dresses, making sure their bows looked beautiful and their ruffles were just right. George typed another text message on Kipper's phone and left a new envelope beside it. Then they locked the door with Kipper's lock and set everything up so it would work again the same way tomorrow.

"Are you sure we can't stay here and watch all the fun?" asked Harold.

"We better not," said George. "Things are about to get even *uglier*!"

THINGS GET EVEN UGLIER

When wrestling practice ended at 4:30, Kipper's friends rushed to their lockers and turned on their mobile phones. As they had suspected, there was another text from Kipper.

By the time Kipper got to his locker, he
knew something was wrong.

"What?" he yelled at his friends. "What
NOW?"

"Sorry, dude," said Loogie, "but we don't
wanna play *dress up* with you!"

"Yeah, *Princess*," said Finkstein. The three
thugs chuckled.

Kipper grabbed Bugg's mobile phone and
read the message.

"I-I DID NOT WRITE THIS!" Kipper yelled.
"And I DON'T have any *DRESSES* in my
locker, either! I can *PROVE* it!"

Kipper unlocked his locker and opened the
door. . .

. . .revealing three of the prettiest dresses anyone had ever seen.

Kipper's friends started laughing as he closed the door and checked to make sure he had opened the right locker.

"*SOMEBODY* IS MESSING WITH ME," screamed Kipper. He tore the dresses out of his locker and whipped them to the floor.

"Maybe you're just getting in touch with your feminine side," said Loogie. Kipper's three friends burst into hysterical laughter.

"Laugh it up, chumps!" yelled Kipper, as he searched the top shelf of his locker. Sure enough, there was another envelope. He ripped it open and read the message out loud:

THERE IS NO ESCAPE!
Signed, Wedgie Magee

Kipper's friends stopped laughing and looked at the note.

"Dude," said Bugg, "I think you really DID get cursed!"

"At least it's a funny curse," said Loogie.

CHAPTER 22

WEDNESDAY

Another day, another awesome lunch for George and Harold and their classmates. The Piqua Pizza Palace had even delivered salads and breadsticks, and the kindergartners had never been happier.

At the end of the day, when wrestling practice was over, Kipper's three friends dashed back to their lockers as fast as they could to see what bizarre thing Kipper was going to do next. They were not disappointed.

Kipper was already angry when he reached his locker. He knew something was not right.

"What?" he yelled at his friends. "WHAT ARE YOU GUYS LAUGHING ABOUT?!!?"

"Dude," said Loogie, "can I bring a teddy bear to your tea party, or is it just for dollies only?" The three thugs burst out laughing.

Kipper grabbed Loogie's mobile phone and read the message.

"I—DID—NOT—WRITE—THIS!" Kipper screamed wildly. "And I DON'T have any DOLLS in my locker, either!"

Kipper grabbed the key from the chain around his neck, unlocked his padlock and threw the locker door open with a mighty crash.

About twenty dolls tumbled out of the
locker and fell into a pile at Kipper's feet.

Kipper's friends each took a few steps back.
They weren't sure whether to keep laughing
or start running. Kipper did nothing at first.
He just stood there looking down at the
mountain of dolls at his feet.

Then he began breathing heavily as he started to twitch. The trembling originated at Kipper's feet, making its way slowly up his legs. By the time it reached Kipper's upper body, he was shaking like a volcano that was about to explode. Kipper squeezed his fists into tight knots of fury as he raised his right foot and began kicking the dolls.

"I HATE YOU! I HATE YOU! I HATE YOU!" Kipper screamed, as he punted his pretty dollies up and down the hallway.

Kipper's friends had never seen a freak-out quite like this. Kipper grabbed two of the bigger dolls and started swinging them around and around, smashing them against his locker door and just about anything

else that was nearby. Then came the tearing
and the biting and the stomping and the
decapitating. Loogie, Bugg, and Finkstein
decided it might be a good time to start
running.

Kipper's berserk-a-thon lasted about fifteen minutes. Finally, he collapsed, exhausted, in a pile of fluffy polyester filling, shredded dolly dresses and tiny plastic arms, legs and heads. Kipper just sat there, breathing slowly for a long time and staring at nothing. Then, Kipper thought of something. It was as if he had finally figured out the mysteries of the ages.

He stood up and grabbed his padlock from the top of his locker. Carefully, he turned it over and over again in his hands, studying it very closely.

"A-*HA*!" he exclaimed.

CHAPTER 23

THURSDAY

Things were back to normal on Thursday. Kipper stood in front of the school and made every kindergartner hand over their lunch money. "Things are gonna change around here," Kipper told the children. "Starting tomorrow, your taxes are going UP! You kids are gonna have to pay me four bucks a day, or it's *WEDGIE TIME*!"

Kipper's three thugs watched the shakedowns from a distance. Finally, they approached Kipper nervously.

"Dude," said Loogie. "What are you doing, man?"

"I'm taking back what's rightfully *MINE*!" said Kipper.

"But aren't you afraid of the ghost of Wedgie Magee?" asked Bugg.

"There is no ghost of Wedgie Magee, you moron!" yelled Kipper. "It's all a set-up! I figured it out last night! Somebody has been

picking my padlock and putting stuff in my locker!"

"But who would do that?" asked Loogie.

"The same person who has been writing those stupid text messages on my mobile phone!" said Kipper. "But it's all going to end today!"

"How?" asked Loogie.

"I got a NEW padlock!" said Kipper. He reached into his pocket and pulled out a brand-new Supa-Doopa Combo Lock 2000. "This thing is totally *pick-proof*," said Kipper.

The four thugs walked into the school and headed for the lockers. Kipper unlocked his old padlock and threw it into the garbage can, along with the key around his sweaty neck. Then Kipper put his all-new *pick-proof* combination padlock on his locker and clicked it shut.

"Let's see somebody try to mess with me NOW!" Kipper sneered.

At noon, when the pizza delivery guy showed up with lunch for the kindergartners, Kipper stopped him in the hallway.

"We'll take those pizzas," said Kipper.

"But I'm supposed to deliver them to the kindergartners," said the delivery guy.

"We'll do it for you," said Kipper.

"Sorry," said the delivery guy, "but I've got strict instructions from Wedgie Magee to—"

"Oh, Uncle Benny!" Kipper yelled.

545

Mr Krupp came bounding up the hallway.

Boom! Boom! Boom! Boom! Boom!

"What seems to be the problem, Kipper?" he asked.

"This guy is delivering pizzas to the kindergartners," said Kipper. "Is he *allowed* to do that?"

"Absolutely NOT," said Principal Krupp. "Those kids are on diets!"

"See?" said Kipper to the delivery guy. "Now *gimme* those!"

Kipper's thugs took the pizzas and the pop away from the delivery guy. They brought it straight to the kindergartners' table in the cafeteria and started stuffing their faces.

"MMMMMM!" said Kipper to the hungry kindergartners. "This pizza sure is *tasty*!" The four barbarians devoured eight whole pizzas between them and finished off fourteen cans of pop. Then they sold all of their leftovers to some of the other students.

"Too bad the *KINDERGARTNERS* can't buy any." Kipper laughed. "But they don't have any money, do they?"

George and Harold were heartbroken. They had already seen Kipper's new padlock and noticed that it never left Kipper's hands when he unlocked it – not even for a second.

"Well," said Harold sadly, "I guess the jig is up!"

"Nothing's over till *WE* say it's over," said George. "We've got to think of something else – *and quick*!"

CHAPTER 24

FOAMY, WHITE ECTOPLASM

After school, George and Harold waited until the hallways were empty. Then they opened their secret stall in the boys' bathroom. George had an idea. He climbed up on the stilts, and Harold pulled the trousers all the way up to the top of George's head. Then George tried walking around, looking out the zipper hole with one eye.

"Well," said George. "How do I look?"

"I'm not sure," said Harold. "You kinda look like an afro with legs."

"Hmmmm. . ." said George, as he peeked at himself in the bathroom mirror. "I think I'm going to need a haircut!" George's idea would have to wait until tomorrow.

Fortunately, the two boys had a backup plan. George and Harold ran to the convenience store up the street and bought four cans of shaving cream and a box of bendy straws. Then they hurried back to the school.

"We're gonna have to work fast," said Harold. The two boys opened their box of bendy straws and pushed a straw over the spray nozzle of each can of shaving cream. Then George stuck a straw up Kipper's locker vent and began spraying.

Harold took another can, stuck the straw up the vent of Loogie's locker and started squirting.

After a few minutes, George's and Harold's cans were empty. They then took two more cans and did the same thing to Bugg's and Finkstein's lockers.

George and Harold hid the empty shaving cream cans in their secret bathroom stall. Then they ran out the back door of the school towards the football field, screaming their heads off.

The cheerleaders, who were just finishing their practice, saw George and Harold running around like lunatics. "What's wrong, little boys?" asked one of the cheerleaders.

"W-w-w-we just saw a g-g-g-ghost!" cried
George.

"Y-y-yeah!" cried Harold. "He was in the
hallway over by the lockers!"

The cheerleaders were frightened. "What
did he look like?" they asked.

"He was invisible," cried George. "But he
left a trail of foamy, white ectoplasm wherever
he went!"

The cheerleaders screamed. They were
terrified, but they were also very curious.

The girls huddled together in a tight,
shivering group as they tiptoed into the school
to see for themselves. Everything looked
normal, but they still screamed a lot anyway.
One of them pushed the button on the
drinking fountain, and when water squirted
out, they all screamed some more.

"What's going on?" yelled Kipper, who had just gotten out of wrestling practice with his buddies.

The cheerleaders screamed again. "Th-th-there's a ghost up here!" cried Wendy Swan. "Some little kids saw it! It was leaving foamy, white ectoplasm everywhere."

"That's crazy!" Kipper yelled. "Ghosts aren't for real!" He and his buddies laughed arrogantly as they unlocked their lockers and opened the doors.

Suddenly, four giant waves of foamy, white shaving cream splashed out into the hallway.

"FOAMY, WHITE ECTOPLASM!" yelled the cheerleaders. They screamed and ran for their lives.

"Ectoplasm?" cried Bugg. "I've heard of that! Th-th-that's *ghost juice*!"

"I-I-I got *ghost juice* on my trousers!" Loogie wailed, as he burst into tears.

"Get it OFF! Get it OFF! *Get it OFF!*" screamed Finkstein, as he jumped around frantically swatting at the shaving cream that covered his legs. *"I HATE GHOST JUICE!!!"*

"THERE'S
NO SUCH THING AS
GHOSTS!" Kipper yelled,
but it was no use. Loogie,
Bugg, and Finkstein slammed
their lockers and screamed in horror
as they slipped and slid in the foamy, white
ectoplasm. The three terrified thugs tumbled
down the stairs, tripping and pushing and
elbowing each other as they struggled to glide
out of the front door.

Kipper was at his wit's end. He plopped down on the floor in the middle of the hallway and curled up into a shivering ball.

"UNCLE BENNY!" he wailed.

As usual, Mr Krupp came running down the hallway.

Boom! Boom! Boom! Boom! Boom!

"What's wrong? What's wrong?" yelled Mr Krupp.

Kipper showed Mr Krupp the ectoplasm and told him the whole terrifying story.

"That's a bunch of *BUNK*!" yelled Mr Krupp. "This isn't ectoplasm, it's shaving cream! I use this same brand myself!"

"Shaving cream?" said Kipper. "B-But how did it get inside our lockers?"

"Well, somebody probably sprayed it through those vents on the door!" Mr Krupp said. "It's the oldest trick in the book!"

Kipper studied the vents on the locker door as his passive, fearful expression slowly turned into a venomous visage of violence. Now Kipper was *REALLY* mad.

CHAPTER 25

THURSDAY AFTERNOON

That afternoon at Harold's house, George and Harold wrote and illustrated a brand-new comic book. When they were done, they scanned each page and printed out four copies on Harold's printer.

The comic book had to look very old, so
they took a large bowl outside and filled it
with water. Harold added two handfuls of dirt
and stirred eight tablespoons of instant coffee
crystals into the water. George carefully tore
the edges of each page, then crumpled them
all up into little balls and soaked them in the
giant bowl of filthy water.

Once each page was completely soaked, the two friends carefully clipped them up in the garage so they could dry overnight.

"What on earth are you boys doing?" said Harold's mother.

"It's for school," said Harold.

"Oh," said Harold's mom.

Next, the two boys went back inside Harold's house.

"Now we've gotta order some pizzas!" said George.

"Order pizzas?" cried Harold. "Why? Kipper's just going to steal them again!"

"That's what I'm counting on," George said with a devilish grin.

George picked up the telephone and spoke with the manager of Piqua Pizza Palace.

"I'd like to order four pizzas for tomorrow," said George. "What's the hottest kind of chilli peppers you guys have? *Ghost* chilli peppers? Hmmmm. Can we get *double* ghost chilli peppers on each pizza? Cool!"

After the pizzas were ordered, it was time
for George's haircut. Harold went to the closet
and found the clippers and scissors his mom
always used to cut his hair. Harold had never
cut anybody's hair before, but he was more
than happy to give it a try.

"Just make the top part flat," said George.
"So it won't stick out when I wear those stilt
trousers!"

"I'll do my best," said Harold.

Harold clipped and cut, then he snipped
and shaped. When he was done, George
looked at himself in the mirror.

"I LOOK *AWESOME*!" George exclaimed.
"I'm gonna wear my hair like this from
now on!"

And he always did.

CHAPTER 26

WHEN KIPPER GETS ANGRY — REALLY, REALLY ANGRY...

The next morning, George and Harold's comic book pages were dry enough to staple together. George sprinkled each page with baby powder to make them look dusty and prehistoric.

"Man," said Harold. "These look like they came from the 1980s or something!"

Friday morning at school was turning out to be the worst day ever. All week long, George and Harold had worked to make things better for their fellow kindergartners, but they had only succeeded in turning Kipper and his gang into MONSTERS.

Kipper had told his friends about the shaving-cream prank and now they were really, really angry, too. The four bullies knew somebody was pranking them and they were going to make every kindergartner's life intolerable until they found out who it was.

"HEY! Where's my eight dollars?" Kipper yelled at Donny Shoemyer, who happened to be the first kindergartner he saw on Friday morning.

"I-I thought you said *four* dollars," said Donny.

"I did," said Kipper. "But taxes just went up *again*. And they're gonna stay high until I find out the name of the person who's been pulling pranks on me!"

"I-I-I don't know who it is," said Donny.

"Well, you'd better find out," Kipper growled. "Or I'm gonna stop being such a nice guy to you little twerps!" Kipper grabbed Donny's money while his thugs gave Donny the worst wedgie of his life.

"You owe me four more dollars!" yelled Kipper. "So bring *TWELVE* dollars on Monday, or you're gonna wish you'd never been born!"

The rest of the kindergartners received similar treatment when they tried to enter the school. Unfortunately for them, nobody had any idea who was pranking Kipper and his friends.

At lunchtime, the delivery guy from Piqua Pizza Palace showed up.

"Hey!" shouted Kipper. "How come there's only four pizzas today?"

"That's all Mr Magee ordered," said the delivery guy.

"What a *cheapskate*!" Kipper sneered. "Well, hand 'em over, bub!"

"OK, but I need to give you a warning," said the delivery guy. "These pizzas are really, REALLY HOT."

"They'd *better* be hot!" yelled Kipper. "I *hate* cold pizza!"

Kipper yanked the pizzas out of the delivery guy's hands and headed towards the cafeteria with his friends. They kicked the lunchroom door open and strutted over to the kindergartners' table.

"MMMMM! Look at all the tasty pizza we got!" Kipper said to the hungry kids. "I'll bet you guys are *starving*! Awww, that's so sad."

Kipper, Bugg, Loogie and Finkstein each grabbed a giant slice and crammed it into their mouths. The four bullies smiled obnoxiously as they chewed with wide, revoltingly cavernous mouths that showed every mushy glob of shiny, doughy goo.

"Whew! This pizza's kinda hot," said Finkstein, as he swallowed harshly and wiped some sweat off his forehead.

"Y-yeah," said Loogie. "This pizza is *really* HOT!"

"Ow! Ow! Owowowowow!" cried Kipper. "This pizza is WAY TOO HOT!!!"

"It BURNS! It BURNS!" wailed Bugg, as he stuck out his tongue and tried to blow on it. "Ooo! OOOO! *OOOOOOOO!*"

Suddenly, the bullies' exaggerated smiles morphed into bug-eyed expressions of sheer horror. Quickly, they began wiping off their tongues with their filthy hands, but it was too late. The ghost chillis had already done their damage. Kipper and his terror-stricken buddies stampeded to the drinking fountain, waving their arms and shrieking like a cackle of panicked hyenas. They pushed and shoved each other in a desperate attempt to splash cold water on to their tongues.

Kipper wasn't having much success at the drinking fountain, so he bolted to the milk table. There, he began clawing the tiny half-pint milk cartons open, one after the other and splashing the milk into his face. The other three thugs followed, shoving and jabbing and kicking each other as they tore the tiny cartons with their teeth and sprayed the milk into their gaping, smouldering mouths.

When the milk was gone, the four bullies
dropped to the floor, grunting and wailing and
crying for their mommies as they licked up
all the milk that had spilled during their lacto-
guzzling frenzy. The entire event had been
filmed by about twenty kids on their mobile
phones and the embarrassing videos were all
posted online before the end of lunch break.

Kipper, Bugg, Loogie and Finkstein all
spent the next two hours in the nurse's room,
holding ice packs on their tongues and crying
like toddlers. They started to feel better just
as the school day was ending and wrestling
practice was about to begin.

CHAPTER 27

SOMETHING WEDGIE THIS WAY COMES

At 2:45 P.M., when the final bell rang, George and Harold ran to their secret bathroom stall and grabbed two empty glass jam jars. Then they headed out towards the caretaker's shed.

There were always a ton of spiders back there and George and Harold worked very hard to safely capture as many as they could.

"We gotta hurry," said George. "It looks like it's going to rain!"

Once they had collected about twenty harmless garden spiders each, they ran back upstairs to the lockers in the empty hallway.

Harold held a piece of paper under one of the lower vent slots of Kipper's locker. George opened his glass jam jar and sprinkled some spiders on to the paper as Harold blew softly. About ten spiders gently slid across the paper and through the slot, disappearing into the darkened depths of Kipper's locker. Next they moved on to Loogie's, Bugg's, and Finkstein's lockers, gently blowing an assortment of eight-legged residents into their vents, too.

George and Harold knew that it takes about an hour for a spider to build a completed web. They looked at the clock on the wall and realized they had only forty-four minutes until wrestling practice was over.

"I hope those spiders work fast," said Harold.

"We gotta work fast, too," said George. "There's still lots of stuff to be done!"

The two boys grabbed some supplies and sneaked into the boys' locker room next to the gym. Harold found Kipper's deodorant stick, pulled off the cap, and twisted the dial on the bottom until the deodorant stuck all the way out of the canister. George pulled the thick, white deodorant off and threw it into the garbage can.

Then he opened a package of extra-spicy jalapeño cream cheese and began packing it into the plastic deodorant canister with a spoon.

When the canister was filled, Harold moulded the cream cheese into shape with his fingers, then popped the cap back on. George put the deodorant back in Kipper's gym locker next to his soap and his towel, while Harold started working on Loogie's deodorant. It took about thirty minutes, but soon George and Harold had transformed all four of the bullies' deodorant sticks into jalapeño cream cheese applicators.

Once everything was back where it belonged, George and Harold rushed to their secret stall in the boys' bathroom. Time was running out.

George climbed on to his stilts as Harold gathered the ancient-looking comics and an old walkie-talkie. Quickly, the two friends sneaked out to the hallway and got to work.

Harold slid a comic book through one of the lower vent slots of each bully's locker while George placed the walkie-talkie on top of the lockers and pumped up the volume. They finished just as wrestling practice ended.

Dark clouds were beginning to gather outside and a distant thunder could be heard rumbling miles away. A terrible storm was coming.

Meanwhile, back in the locker room, Kipper and his thugs changed their clothes, smeared on some deodorant and strutted out to their lockers. Lightning was beginning to flash outside, filling the school windows with crackling bursts of fluorescence.

The four hooligans unlocked their locker doors and swung them open, just as a deafening thunderclap rocked the school hallway.

CRASH!!!

The terror-stricken tyrants stared in horrified astonishment at their spiderweb-caked compartments.

Loogie, who had a severely intense fear of spiders, was the first one to freak out.

"L-l-l-lockers! H-h-h-Haunted! S-s-s-spiders!" was all he could manage to verbalize as an earsplitting smash of thunder rattled the school. The four ruffians shrieked in panic.

Loogie was losing it. He flicked his hands wildly as he stood in place, leaning from side to side, impulsively raising one knee to his chest, and then the other. "We gotta get out of here, dudes!" he sobbed. "Seriously, we gotta get out of here, dudes. *SERIOUSLY*, DUDES! We *GOTTA* get out of here! DUDES!!! *DUDES!!!*"

"Just a doggone minute," Kipper protested. "What's this?" He reached carefully into his web-choked locker and pulled out an ancient-looking comic book.

"I don't know," said Finkstein. "But I got one, too."

"Me, too," said Bugg.

Loogie would have added that he also had one in his locker, but he had become too frightened to speak. All he could manage was short bursts of screams as he danced around the hallway, twitching and jerking like a demented chicken.

Kipper opened the antique comic and began to read aloud as turbulent thunder rumbled around them.

OW! How come myFood tastes Hot and SPISY all uva suden?
Its Becuze you are Hawnted, sun
Fire
I am the Hawnted pants of Wedgie MAgee
crash
Yaaaa
This is For steeLing money.

BONiS SeCKSHON:

✳ How to tell if you ✳
    Got Cursed:

① You start ackting all
    weerd and stuff.
② You want to play with
    doLLys and dresses and
    ~~f~~ BraseLits.
③ You get ecktoplasim on
    your stuff (and spiders too).
④ awesome Food Like pizza
    tasts all hot and burns
    your mouth and stuff.
⑤ your ~~and~~ armpits get ~~all~~
    all burny and stuff.

How to undo this curse

you must undo all the bad
stuff you did and never ~~~~
pick on nobody ever again!

CHAPTER 29

THE PERFECT STORM

It was getting dark now and the storm outside was intensifying.

The four bullies stared in knee-melting terror at the dusty, ancient comic in Kipper's trembling hands. Their mouths hung open in shock, but they were too afraid to move.

Finally, Finkstein began frantically scratching his sweat-soaked armpits.

"Dudes," he blurted, "we're *DEAD*, man. It's *OVER*!! Game OVER, man!"

Bugg began to cry. "My *pits* are burning, man," he sobbed. "I think I got *the curse*!"

"M-m-m-me, too," Loogie squeaked, as tears poured down his face.

Kipper looked into the quivering eyes of his three terrified friends. His armpits were burning as well, but he was too frightened to admit it.

Suddenly, a deafening blast of thunder shook the building. The lightbulbs in the school flickered twice and the bullies held each other and sobbed uncontrollably.

Inside the bathroom, George and Harold could hear their arch-enemies shrieking out in the hallway and the two friends tried as hard as they could to keep from laughing. They both knew if they started, they'd never be able to stop. Harold picked up his walkie-talkie and pressed the "transmit" button.

The toy walkie-talkie on top of the lockers clicked with a crackle of static.

"I am the haunted trousers of Wedgie Magee!" whispered Harold over the tiny speaker.

"HEY!" cried Kipper. "DID-DID YOU GUYS HEAR THAT?"

"I am coming for yooooooou!" Harold whispered.

"No! No! No! No! No! No! NOOOO!" screamed Loogie, who was now running around in small circles, punching his head with his fists (for some strange reason).

Lightning exploded again and the hallways rumbled with thunder. The four bullies had now become completely unhinged. Bugg dropped to the floor and curled up into a shivering ball, crying out for his mother to come and save him.

"L-L-LEAVE US ALONE," Kipper screamed, swinging his fists in the air. "WE'RE *SORRY*!"

Mr Krupp was in the middle of a teachers'
meeting all the way on the other end of the
building when he heard the screaming.

"It sounds like Kipper's freaking out
again," he growled, slamming his fist on the
table. "And I'm going to get to the bottom
of it!" He got up from the meeting and
stomped out of the room.

604

Kipper and his friends heard the pounding sounds of stomping feet coming from the other side of the school building. **Boom!** *Boom!* **Boom!** *Boom!* **Boom!** *Boom!* **Boom!** *Boom!* **Boom!** *Boom!* The stomping got louder and louder, and closer and closer.

"Let's hide in the bathroom!" screamed Loogie, through his tears. Immediately, the four frightened friends scrambled for the bathroom door.

Inside the bathroom, George and Harold were still getting ready for their final prank. Harold steadied the wooden stilts while George pulled the tall pair of trousers up over his head. The two kindergartners didn't know they were about to be ambushed.

"I can't see," said George.

"Here," said Harold. "Let me –"

Suddenly, the bathroom door crashed open and the terrified bullies tumbled inside. They looked at Harold holding on to the giant pair of trousers in front of them. Lightning pierced the darkened clouds and everyone froze. The stomping footsteps came closer and closer.
Boom! *Boom!* Boom! *Boom!* Boom! *Boom!* Boom! *Boom!*

"W-w-what are you doing with those
trousers, kid?" cried Kipper.

Harold couldn't think of a thing to say.
It wasn't supposed to happen like this. They
weren't ready. For a split second, Harold
saw his entire life flash before his eyes. He
and George were going to get caught. Their
lives were about to end. The footsteps in the
hallway got even louder.

Boom! *Boom!* **Boom!** *Boom!*
Boom! *Boom!*

608

George knew they were in trouble. He couldn't see, but he grasped the stilts anyway and took a blind, wobbly step forward. The bullies beheld what appeared to be a pair of trousers walking by themselves. They grasped each other and shrieked in earsplitting horror.

"Get away from those trousers, kid," cried Bugg. *"GET AWAY FROM THOSE TROUSERS!"*

Then, as if an angel had whispered it into his ear, Harold thought of the perfect thing to say.

"What trousers?" he asked.

BOOM!

Suddenly, time seemed to stand still.

BOOM!

The four bullies stepped back in horror.

BOOM!

Their eyes grew impossibly wide.

BOOM!

They opened their mouths to scream. . .

BOOM!

. . .but not a sound came out.

BOOM!

George took another step towards the bullies . . .

BOOM!

. . .as they clawed at the wall behind them.

BOOM!

Then the lightning flashed again. . .

. . .and everything went dark.

The terrible storm had knocked out a power

line nearby and the school was now completely

black. Kipper and his thugs scrambled over

each other, desperately trying to make their

way through the bathroom door.

Mr Krupp was to be their next obstacle.

He had finally reached the lockers when the

lights went out. His elephantine footsteps had

stopped cold and he stood in the darkness,

breathing heavily and sweating abundantly.

When the four squealing defcncts many

tumbled out of the bathroom and bolted down

the dark hallway, they smashed right into him.

Nobody would be able to blame the bullies

for what they did next. In their profoundly

petrified perceptions, they must have believed

that Mr Krupp was some kind of giant, wet,

fleshy monster – and they treated him as such.

Screeching and wailing in the darkness, they

kicked and clobbered the warm, wet, bulbous

creature with all the strength they had.

The four distressed delinquents then
tumbled down the stairs and shoved their way
through the back door of the school.
As they ran across the football field towards
their homes, something about Kipper and
his friends changed for ever. They would
never again be the same despicable bullies
they once were.

CHAPTER 30

THE WONDERFUL, HAPPY, INCREDIBLY DELIGHTFUL ENDING

Monday morning was a very stressful time for Donny Shoemyer. He had not been able to scrape up the twelve dollars he owed Kipper, so he was trying to sneak into the school through the back door without being noticed. Kipper saw him.

"Hey, kid!" yelled Kipper. "Wait up! I got something for ya!"

Donny pulled at the door, but it was locked. He kept pulling and pulling anyway as Kipper approached.

"I got some money for you," said Kipper nervously. He reached into his pocket and handed Donny a crinkled five dollar bill.

Donny stopped pulling at the door and looked at the money in Kipper's hand. "Is this a trick?" Donny asked.

"No," Kipper said. "I'm really sorry I took money from you, kid. I'm gonna pay ya back every dollar as soon as I can, OK?"

"Umm . . . OK," said Donny. He took the five dollar bill from Kipper's hand and rushed to the front door of the school. His morning had turned out a *LOT* different than he had expected.

All around the school, the other kindergartners were having similar experiences.

Finkstein was not only passing out money, he was also offering to carry every kindergartner's book bag to class. Bugg was handing out cash and free bubble gum, and Loogie was distributing dollars AND letting the kindergartners give him as many wedgies as they wanted.

Kipper and his three friends eventually paid back all the money they had stolen, and they never bullied another person for as long as they lived.

Once George and Harold were certain that their enemies had truly been reformed, they called off the vengeful wrath of Wedgie Magee. The terrifying curse had finally been lifted, everyone was happy and all was well with the world.

I'd like to tell you that this is the end of our story. I really would – but I can't. Because this wonderful, happy, incredibly delightful ending is what was *supposed* to happen . . . not what actually *did* happen.

Remember back in Chapter 8 when Tippy Tinkletrousers was fighting Captain Underpants and he accidentally froze his giant Robo-Legs to the school's football field? Well, if you'll recall, Tippy got out of this jam by zapping himself back in time exactly five years earlier.

Now, see if you can guess which night occurred exactly *five years earlier*. If you guessed the night of the terrible thunderstorm that for ever changed the lives of Kipper and his buddies, you'd be correct.

Unfortunately, by some wild and tragic coincidence, Tippy sent himself and his gigantic Robo-Trousers back in time to the very moment when Kipper and his friends were running across the football field towards their homes.

Ignoring the cautious wisdom of the Banana Cream Pie Paradox, Tippy's reckless journey back through time would end up making one small, seemingly insignificant change. And this one teeny, tiny, itsy-bitsy change would eventually destroy all hopes for the future of our civilization.

As much as I hate to do it, let's go back to the darkened hallway of that fateful, stormy night and find out what *REALLY* happened.

The four distressed delinquents then tumbled down the stairs and shoved their way through the back door of the school. As they ran across the football field towards their homes, something about Kipper and his friends changed for ever. They would never again be the same despicable bullies they once were.

CHAPTER 31

THE TERRIBLE, SAD, INCREDIBLY HORRIFYING ENDING

Suddenly, out of nowhere, a ball of blue lightning appeared in front of them. It grew bigger and bigger until it exploded in a blinding flash.

And there, where the ball of lightning had
been, stood a giant pair of robotic trousers.

"Boy, that was a close one," said Tippy from inside the depths of his giant Robo-Trousers. "Captain Underpants is a lot stronger than I thought!"

Tippy unzipped the zipper of his time-travelling trousers and looked out at the world of five years ago. He saw the raging thunderstorm and the four sixth graders who stood trembling beneath his giant, robotic feet.

"Hey," shouted Tippy. "What's wrong with you kids? You look like you've just seen a ghost!"

"IT'S-IT'S-IT'S THE H-H-HAUNTED T-T-T-TROUSERS OF W-W-WEDGIE M-M-M-MAGEE!" screamed Finkstein, pointing up at Tippy's gigantic, darkened silhouette. Kipper and his buddies screamed so loud and so high, only dogs could hear them.

What happened next is what psychologists commonly refer to as "Going Cuckoo for Cocoa Puffs". The four sixth graders fell to their knees, shaking, twitching, and uttering complete nonsense as their fragile, eggshell minds began to shatter.

"B-B-Bubba bobba hob-hobba-hobba wah-wah!" cried Kipper, as he frantically slapped himself in the face again and again.

Bugg tore off his clothes and began dancing the hula while singing "I'm a Little Teapot" as loudly as he could.

Loogie started digging a hole in the ground with his teeth, gobbling up enormous fistfuls of dirt and worms. And poor Finkstein just laughed maniacally, happily banging his head into the grass over and over and over and over and over.

LEFT HAND HERE

BULLIES GO
BANANAS!

RIGHT
THUMB
HERE

BULLIES GO
BANANAS!

"Boy," said Tippy, "kids sure were weird five years ago." He quickly reset the controllers of his Tinkle-Time Travelometer to "Four Years in da Future" and pressed the "Away We Go!" button.

Suddenly, giant sparks of blue lightning shot out from the Robo-Trousers. Several special-effects-filled moments later, a blinding flash lit up the sky, and Tippy and his Robo-Trousers disappeared.

The next day, the four troubled sixth graders were admitted to the Piqua Valley Home for the Reality-Challenged. An investigation into their mental breakdowns led police straight to Mr Krupp, whose bruised and battered body made everyone VERY suspicious. The cops naturally assumed that Mr Krupp was somehow behind all of this insanity.

Although no formal charges were filed against Mr Krupp, everyone blamed him anyway. Mr Krupp got fired a few weeks later, and he never worked as an elementary school principal again.

CHAPTER 32

FOUR YEARS LATER. . .

Four years later, a giant sphere of blue lightning appeared on what used to be an elementary school football field. Soon, the sphere exploded in a blinding flash of light, leaving Tippy and his gigantic Robo-Trousers behind.

Tippy peeked out of the zipper and discovered that Earth had been destroyed.

He crawled out of his giant Robo-Trousers and shuffled through the shattered city, inspecting the chaos. All around him, the landscape was littered with massive moon rocks, skeletal skyscrapers and torn-up toilets.

"What the heck happened here?" Tippy cried.

When the morning sun rose above the horizon, Tippy finally saw a sign of life. A little preschooler was walking up a burning boulevard with his mother.

"Hey, kid," yelled Tippy. "What happened here? How did Earth get destroyed?"

"Well," said the little boy, "a few weeks ago, some guy in a diaper blew up the moon and tried to take over the world. But a week later, a bunch of Talking Toilets attacked the city and ate him up. Then, a week after that, a spaceship landed on top of the elementary school and all the kids got turned into giant evil zombie nerds!"

"I sure wish you would stop obsessing over such foolish nonsense," the boy's mother said.

"But what about Captain Underpants?" asked Tippy.

"Who's that?" said the boy.

"He's that fat, bald superhero," said Tippy. "You know, the guy with the underwear and the red cape? What happened to him?"

"I've never seen anyone like that," said the little boy.

Suddenly, Tippy realized what a terrible mistake he had made. Somehow he'd changed things in the past, which had resulted in the destruction of both Captain Underpants *AND* Earth.

"I must go back and undo what I did," cried Tippy. "I must go back in time to SAVE Captain Underpants!"

"Quickly, little boy," screamed Tippy, "tell me everything you know about these zombie nerds who have taken over the world!"

"Well," said the little boy, "they're really strong – and they're really powerful!"

"Yes, yes," said Tippy. "What *else* are they?"

"They're right behind you," said the boy.

Tippy turned and looked up. There, standing behind him, were two of the biggest, evilest-looking zombie nerds anyone had ever seen.

One of the zombie nerds raised his foot above Tippy's head.

"NOOOOO!" screamed Tippy. "You can't kill me! I'm the only chance this world has of ever returning to normal!"

CHAPTER 34

THE END (OF THE WORLD AS WE KNOW IT)

When the horrible zombie nerd raised his foot again, all that remained was a red squishy stain.

And that, dear readers, is the unfortunate end of the Captain Underpants saga.

Dr Diaper blew up the moon, the Talking Toilets attacked and zombie nerds took over Earth. Captain Underpants wasn't there to save the world, because Mr Krupp wasn't there to get hypnotized by George and Harold.

All of the epic adventures we've come to know and love never actually happened. And now, the only chance of making things right again has just been obliterated.

It is with great sadness that I must tell you: This is the final chapter of the last Captain Underpants epic novel. There will be no more Captain Underpants adventures. . .

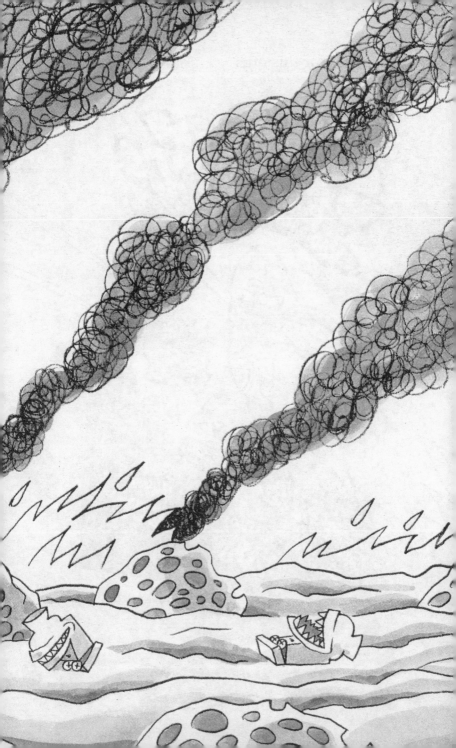

. . .except for this one: